JESSE F. BONE
RESURRECTED

Selected Stories of Jesse Franklin Bone

By Jesse F. Bone
Edited by Greg Fowlkes

Includes the Special Bonus Story
AND NOW A MESSAGE . . .
By Greg Fowlkes

JESSE F. BONE RESURRECTED

Selected Stories of Jesse Franklin Bone

© 2011 Resurrected Press
www.ResurrectedPress.com

Published by Intrepid Ink, LLC

Intrepid Ink, LLC provides full publishing services to authors of fiction and non-fiction books, eBooks and websites. From editing to formatting, to publishing, to marketing, Intrepid Ink gets your creative works into the hands of the people who want to read them.
Find out more at www.IntrepidInk.com.

ISBN 13: 978-1-935774-98-3

Printed in the United States of America

FOREWORD

There isn't a lot of biographical information readily available on Jesse Franklin Bone. At the time this is written, there is no Wikipedia entry, no internet bibliography, only links to some of his works that are in the public domain. In the end, like any author, what we have to judge him on our his works.

The eight stories contained in this collection span a period of four years from 1958 to 1962. They were originally published in some of the more well known magazines of the period, *Galaxy*, *Amazing Science Fiction Stories*, *Analog* and *IF*. Some are serious, some humorous, but most blend the two in a manner that was typical of much of the science fiction of the era known as "The Golden Age."

The subject matter of these stories is typical of the period, as well, most of them dealing with the interaction of humans and aliens or humans and technology. With the realities of "the space age" still mostly in the future, writers such as Bone were free to use their imagination unconstrained by inconvenient facts to create worlds and races specifically designed to help them make their point or their punch line. I think this is what really made the 50's and early 60's "The Golden Age."

There are certainly better known authors from the period, but Bone's work can hold its own. It is still readable, still enjoyable. What more can we ask of an author. When the concept for this series of books came up, Jesse Franklin Bone's name was one of the first that came to mind for inclusion. I hope that after you read these stories you will agree with that judgement.

Greg Fowlkes
Editor-In-Chief
Resurrected Press
www.ResurrectedPress.com

TABLE OF CONTENTS

ASSASSIN..1

INSIDEKICK 33

THE ISSAHAR ARTIFACTS 77

NOBLE REDMAN.. 91

TO CHOKE AN OCEAN..................................... 113

A QUESTION OF COURAGE................................. 143

A PRIZE FOR EDIE 171

PANDEMIC 179

BONUS! AND NOW A MESSAGE 203

Assassin

Illustrated by Ed Emsh
Originally Published in *If Worlds of Science Fiction*,
February 1958

The aliens wooed Earth with gifts,
love, patience and peace.
Who could resist them? After all,
no one shoots Santa Claus!

Assassin

The rifle lay comfortably in his hands, a gleaming precision instrument that exuded a faint odor of gun oil and powder solvent. It was a perfect specimen of the gunsmith's art, a semi-automatic rifle with a telescopic sight—a precisely engineered tool that could hurl death with pinpoint accuracy for better than half a mile.

Daniel Matson eyed the weapon with bleak gray eyes, the eyes of a hunter framed in the passionless face of an executioner. His blunt hands were steady as they lifted the gun and tried a dry shot at an imaginary target. He nodded to himself. He was ready. Carefully he laid the rifle down on the mattress which covered the floor of his firing point, and looked out through the hole in the brickwork to the narrow canyon of the street below.

The crowd had thickened. It had been gathering since early morning, and the growing press of spectators had now become solid walls of people lining the street, packed tightly together on the sidewalks. Yet despite the fact that there were virtually no police, the crowd did not overflow into the streets, nor was there any of the pushing crowding impatience that once attended an assemblage of this sort. Instead there was a placid tolerance, a spirit of friendly good will, an ingenuous complaisance that grated on Matson's nerves like the screeching rasp of a file drawn across the edge of thin metal. He shivered uncontrollably. It was hard to be a free man in a world of slaves.

It was a measure of the Aztlan's triumph that only a bare half-dozen police 'copters patrolled the empty skies above the parade route. The aliens had done this—had conquered the world without firing a shot or speaking a word in anger. They had wooed Earth with understanding patience and superlative guile—and Earth had fallen into their hands like a lovesick virgin! There never had been any real opposition, and what there was had been completely ineffective. Most of those who had opposed the aliens were out of circulation, imprisoned in correctional institutions, undergoing rehabilitation. Rehabilitation! a six bit word for dehumanizing. When those poor devils finished their treatment with Aztlan brain-washing techniques, they would be just like these sheep below, with the difference that they would never be able to be anything else. But these other stupid fools crowding the sidewalks, waiting to hail their destruction—these were the ones who must be saved. They—not the martyrs of the underground, were the important part of humanity.

A police 'copter windmilled slowly down the avenue toward his hiding place, the rotating vanes and insect body of the craft starkly outlined against the jagged backdrop of the city's skyline. He laughed soundlessly as the susurrating flutter of the rotor blades beat overhead and died whispering in the distance down the long canyon of the street. His position had been chosen with care, and was invisible from air and ground alike. He had selected it months ago, and had taken considerable pains to conceal its true purpose. But after today concealment wouldn't matter. If things went as he hoped, the place might someday become a shrine. The idea amused him.

Strange, he mused, how events conspire to change a man's career. Seven years ago he had been a respected and important member of that far different sort of crowd which had welcomed the visitors from space. That was a human crowd—half afraid, wholly curious, jostling, noisy, pushing—a teeming swarm that clustered in a thick disorderly ring around the silver disc that lay in the center of the International Airport overlooking Puget Sound. Then—he could have predicted his career. And none of the predictions would have been true—for none included a man with a rifle waiting in a blind for the game to approach within range....

The Aztlan ship had landed early that July morning, dropping silently through the overcast covering International Airport. It settled gently to rest precisely in the center of the junction of the three main runways of the field, effectively tying up the transcontinental and transoceanic traffic. Fully five hundred feet in diameter, the giant ship squatted massively on the runway junction, cracking and buckling the thick concrete runways under its enormous weight.

By noon, after the first skepticism had died, and the unbelievable TV pictures had been flashed to their waiting audience, the crowd began to gather. All through that hot July morning they came, increasing by the minute as farther outlying districts poured their curious into the Airport. By early afternoon, literally hundreds of millions of eyes were watching the great ship over a world-wide network of television stations which cancelled their regular programs to give their viewers an uninterrupted view of the enigmatic craft.

By mid-morning the sun had burned off the overcast and was shining with brassy brilliance upon the squads of sweating soldiers from Fort Lewis, and more sweating squads of blue-clad police from the metropolitan area of Seattle-Tacoma. The police and soldiery quickly formed a ring around the ship and cleared a narrow lane around the periphery, and this they maintained despite the increasing pressure of the crowd.

The hours passed and nothing happened. The faint creaking and snapping sounds as the seamless hull of the vessel warmed its space-chilled metal in the warmth of the summer sun were lost in the growing impatience of the crowd. They wanted something to happen. Shouts and catcalls filled the air as more nervous individuals clamored to relieve the tension. Off to one side a small group began to clap their hands rhythmically. The little claque gained recruits, and within moments the air was riven by the thunder of thousands of palms meeting in unison. Frightened the crowd might be, but greater than fear was the desire to see what sort of creatures were inside.

Matson stood in the cleared area surrounding the ship, a position of privilege he shared with a few city and state officials and the high brass from McChord Field, Fort Lewis, and Bremerton Navy Yard. He was one of the bright young men who had chosen Government Service as a career, and who, in these days of science-consciousness had risen rapidly through ability and merit promotions to become the Director of the Office of Scientific Research while still in his early thirties. A dedicated man, trained in the bitter school of ideological survival, he understood what the alien science could mean to this world. Their knowledge would secure peace in whatever terms the possessors cared to name, and Matson intended to make sure that his nation was the one which possessed that knowledge.

He stood beside a tall scholarly looking man named Roger Thornton, who was his friend and incidentally the Commissioner of Police for the Twin City metropolitan area. To a casual eye, their positions should be reversed, for the lean ascetic Thornton looked far more like the accepted idea of a scientist than burly, thick shouldered, square faced Matson, whose every movement shouted Cop.

Matson glanced quizzically at the taller man. "Well, Roger, I wonder how long those birds inside are going to keep us waiting before we get a look at them?"

"You'd be surprised if they really were birds, wouldn't you?" Thornton asked with a faint smile. "But seriously, I hope it isn't too much longer. This mob is giving the boys a bad time." He looked anxiously at the strained line of police and soldiery. "I guess I should have ordered out the night shift and reserves instead of just the riot squad. From the looks of things they'll be needed if this crowd gets any more unruly."

Matson chuckled. "You're an alarmist," he said mildly. "As far as I can see they're doing all right. I'm not worried about them—or the crowd, for that matter. The thing that's bothering me is my feet. I've been standing on 'em for six hours and they're killing me!"

"Mine too," Thornton sighed. "Tell you what I'll do. When this is all over I'll split a bucket of hot water and a pint of arnica with you."

"It's a deal," Matson said.

As he spoke a deep musical hum came from inside the ship, and a section of the rim beside him separated along invisible lines of juncture, swinging downward to form a broad ramp leading upward to a square orifice in the rim of the ship. A bright shadowless light that seemed to come from the metal walls of the opening framed the shape of the star traveller who stood there, rigidly erect, looking over the heads of the section of the crowd before him.

A concerted gasp of awe and admiration rose from the crowd—a gasp that was echoed throughout the entire ring that surrounded the ship. There must be other openings like this one, Matson thought dully as he stared at the being from space. Behind him an Army tank rumbled noisily on its treads as it drove through the crowd toward the ship, the long gun in its turret lifting like an alert finger to point at the figure of the alien.

The stranger didn't move from his unnaturally stiff position. His oddly luminous eyes never wavered from their fixed stare at a point far beyond the outermost fringes of the crowd. Seven feet tall, obviously masculine, he differed from mankind only in minor details. His long slender hands lacked the little finger, and his waist was abnormally small. Other than that, he was human in external appearance. A wide sleeved tunic of metallic fabric covered his upper body, gathered in at his narrow waist by a broad metal belt studded with tiny bosses. The tunic ended halfway between hip and knee, revealing powerfully muscled legs encased in silvery hose. Bright yellow hair hung to his shoulders, clipped short in a square bang across his forehead. His face was long, clean featured and extraordinarily calm—almost godlike in its repose. Matson stared, fascinated. He had the curious impression that the visitor had stepped bodily out of the Middle Ages. His dress and haircut were almost identical with that of a medieval courtier.

The starman raised his hand—his strangely luminous steel gray eyes scanned the crowd—and into Matson's mind came a wave of peaceful calm, a warm feeling of goodwill and brotherhood, an indescribable feeling of soothing relaxation. With an odd sense of shock Matson realized that he was not the only one to experience this. As far back as the farthest hangers-on near the airport gates the tenseness of the waiting crowd relaxed. The effect was amazing! Troops lowered their weapons with shamefaced smiles on their faces. Police relaxed their sweating vigilance. The crowd stirred, moving backward to give its members room. The emotion-charged atmosphere vanished as though it had never been. And a cold chill played icy fingers up the spine of Daniel Matson. He had felt the full impact of the alien's projection, and he was more frightened than he had ever been in his life!

*   *   *   *   *

They had been clever—damnably clever! That initial greeting with its disarming undertones of empathy and innocence had accomplished its purpose. It had emasculated Mankind's natural suspicion of strangers. And their subsequent actions—so beautifully timed—so careful to avoid the slightest hint of evil, had completed what their magnificently staged appearance had begun.

The feeling of trust had persisted. It lasted through quarantine, clearance, the public receptions, and the private meetings with scientists and the heads of government. It had persisted unabated through the entire two months they remained in the Twin City area. The aliens remained as they had been in the beginning—completely unspoiled by the interest shown in them. They remained simple, unaffected, and friendly, displaying an ingenuous innocence that demanded a corresponding faith in return.

Most of their time was spent at the University of Washington, where at their own request they were studied by curious scholars, and in return were given courses in human history and behavior. They were quite frank about their reasons for following such a course of action—according to their spokesman Ixtl they wanted to learn human ways in order to make a better impression when they visited the rest of Mankind. Matson read that blurb in an official press release and laughed cynically. Better impression, hah! They couldn't have done any better if they had an entire corps of public relations specialists assisting them! They struck exactly the right note—and how could they improve on perfection?

From the beginning they left their great ship open and unguarded while they commuted back and forth from the airport to the campus. And naturally the government quickly rectified the second error and took instant advantage of the first. A guard was posted around the ship to keep it clear of the unofficially curious, while the officially curious combed the vessel's interior with a fine tooth comb. Teams of scientists and technicians under Matson's direction swarmed through the ship, searching with the most advanced methods of human science for the secrets of the aliens.

They quickly discovered that while the star travellers might be trusting, they were not exactly fools. There was nothing about the impenetrably shielded mechanisms that gave the slightest clue as to their purpose or to the principles upon which they operated—nor were there any visible controls. The ship was as blankly uncommunicative as a brick wall.

Matson was annoyed. He had expected more than this, and his frustration drove him to watch the aliens closely. He followed them, sat in on their sessions with the scholars at the University, watched them at their frequent public appearances, and came to know them well enough to recognize the microscopic differences that made them individuals. To the casual eye they were as alike as peas in a pod, but Matson could separate Farn from Quicha, and Laz from Acana—and Ixtl—well he would have stood out from the others in any circumstances. But Matson never intruded. He was content to sit in the background and observe.

And what he saw bothered him. They gave him no reason for their appearance on Earth, and whenever the question came up Ixtl parried it adroitly. They were obviously not explorers for they displayed a startling familiarity with Earth's geography and ecology. They were possibly ambassadors, although they behaved like no ambassadors he had ever seen. They might be traders, although what they would trade only God and the aliens knew—and neither party was in a talking mood. Mysteries bothered Matson. He didn't like them. But they could keep their mystery if he could only have the technical knowledge that was concealed beneath their beautifully shaped skulls.

At that, he had to admit that their appearance had come at precisely the right time. No one better than he knew how close Mankind had been to the final war, when the last two major antagonists on Earth were girding their human and industrial power for a final showdown. But the aliens had become a diversion. The impending war was forgotten while men waited to see what was coming next. It was obvious that the starmen had a reason for being here, and until they chose to reveal it, humanity would forget its deadly problems in anticipation of the answer to this delightful puzzle that had come to them from outer space. Matson was thankful for the breathing space, all too well aware that it might be the last that Mankind might have, but the enigma of the aliens still bothered him.

He was walking down the main corridor of the Physics Building on the University campus, wondering as he constantly did about how he could extract some useful knowledge from the aliens when a quiet voice speaking accentless English sounded behind him.

"What precisely do you wish to know, Dr. Matson?" the voice said.

Matson whirled to face the questioner, and looked into the face of Ixtl. The alien was smiling, apparently pleased at having startled him. "What gave you the idea that I wanted to know anything?" he asked.

"You did," Ixtl said. "We all have been conscious of your thoughts for many days. Forgive me for intruding, but I must. Your speculations radiate on such a broad band that we cannot help being aware of them. It has been quite difficult for us to study your customs and history with this high level background noise. We are aware of your interest, but your thoughts are so confused that we have never found questions we could answer. If you would be more specific we would be happy to give you the information which you seek."

"Oh yeah!" Matson thought.

"Of course. It would be to our advantage to have your disturbing speculations satisfied and your fears set at rest. We could accomplish more in a calmer environment. It is too bad that you do not receive as strongly as you transmit. If you did, direct mental contact would convince you that our reasons for satisfying you are good. But you need not fear us, Earthman. We intend you no harm. Indeed, we plan to help you once we learn enough to formulate a proper program."

"I do not fear you," Matson said—knowing that he lied.

"Perhaps not consciously," Ixtl said graciously, "but nevertheless fear is in you. It is too bad—and besides," he continued with a faint smile "it is very uncomfortable.

Your glandular emotions are quite primitive, and very disturbing."

"I'll try to keep them under control," Matson said dryly.

"Physical control is not enough. With you there would have to be mental control as well. Unfortunately you radiate much more strongly than your fellow men, and we are unable to shut you out without exerting considerable effort that could better be employed elsewhere." The alien eyed Matson speculatively. "There you go again," he said. "Now you're angry."

Matson tried to force his mind to utter blankness, and the alien smiled at him. "It does some good—but not much," he said. "Conscious control is never perfect."

"Well then, what can I do?"

"Go away. Your range fortunately is short."

Matson looked at the alien. "Not yet," he said coldly. "I'm still looking for something."

"Our technology," Ixtl nodded. "I know. However I can assure you it will be of no help to you. You simply do not have the necessary background. Our science is based upon a completely different philosophy from yours."

To Matson the terms were contradictory.

"Not as much as you think," Ixtl continued imperturbably. "As you will find out, I was speaking quite precisely." He paused and eyed Matson thoughtfully. "It seems as though the only way to remove your disturbing presence is to show you that our technology is of no help to you. I will make a bargain with you. We shall show you our machines, and in return you will stop harassing us. We will do all in our power to make you understand; but whether you do or do not, you will promise to leave and allow us to continue our studies in peace. Is that agreeable?"

Matson swallowed the lump in his throat. Here it was—handed to him on a silver platter—and suddenly he wasn't sure that he wanted it!

"It is," he said. After all, it was all he could expect.

They met that night at the spaceship. The aliens, tall, calm and cool; Matson stocky, heavy-set and sweating. The contrast was infernally sharp, Matson thought. It was as if a primitive savage were meeting a group of nuclear physicists at Los Alamos. For some unknown reason he felt ashamed that he had forced these people to his wishes. But the aliens were pleasant about it. They took the imposition in their usual friendly way.

"Now," Ixtl said. "Exactly what do you want to see—to know?"

"First of all, what is the principle of your space drive?"

"There are two," the alien said. "The drive that moves this ship in normal space time is derived from Lurgil's Fourth Order equations concerning the release of subatomic energy in a restricted space time continuum. Now don't protest! I know you know nothing of Lurgil, nor of Fourth Order equations. And while I can show you the mathematics, I'm afraid they will be of little help. You see, our Fourth Order is based upon a process which you would call Psychomathematics and that is something I am sure you have not yet achieved."

Matson shook his head. "I never heard of it," he admitted.

"The second drive operates in warped space time," Ixtl continued, "hyperspace in your language, and its theory is much more difficult than that of our normal drive, although its application is quite simple, merely involving apposition of congruent surfaces of hyper and normal space at stress points in the ether where high gravitational fields balance. Navigation in hyperspace is done by electronic computer—somewhat more advanced models than yours. However, I can't give you the basis behind the hyperspace drive." Ixtl smiled depreciatingly. "You see, I don't know them myself. Only a few of the most advanced minds of Aztlan can understand. We merely operate the machines."

Matson shrugged. He had expected something like this. Now they would stall him off about the machines after handing him a fast line of double-talk.

"As I said," Ixtl went on, "there is no basis for understanding. Still, if it will satisfy you, we will show you our machines—and the mathematics that created them although I doubt that you will learn anything more from them than you have from our explanation."

"I could try," Matson said grimly.

"Very well," Ixtl replied.

He led the way into the center of the ship where the seamless housings stood, the housings that had baffled some of the better minds of Earth. Matson watched while the star men proceeded to be helpful. The housings fell apart at invisible lines of juncture, revealing mechanisms of baffling simplicity, and some things that didn't look like machines at all. The aliens stripped the strange devices and Ixtl attempted to explain. They had anti-gravity, forcefields, faster than light drive, and advanced design computers that could be packed in a suitcase. There were weird devices whose components seemed to run out of sight at crazily impossible angles, other things that rotated frictionlessly, suspended in fields of pure force, and still others which his mind could not envisage even after his eyes had seen them. All about him lay the evidence of a science so advanced and alien that his brain shrank from the sight, refusing to believe such things existed. And their math was worse! It began where Einstein left off and went off at an incomprehensible tangent that involved psychology and ESP. Matson was lost after the first five seconds!

Stunned, uncomprehending and deflated, he left the ship. An impression that he was standing with his toe barely inside the door of knowledge became a conscious certainty as he walked slowly to his car. The wry thought crossed his mind that if the aliens were trying to convince him of his abysmal ignorance, they had succeeded far beyond their fondest dreams!

They certainly had! Matson thought grimly as he selected five cartridges from the box lying beside him. In fact they had succeeded too well. They had turned his deflation into antagonism, his ignorance into distrust. Like a savage, he suspected what he could not understand. But unlike the true primitive, the emotional distrust didn't interfere with his ability to reason or to draw logical inferences from the data which he accumulated. In attempting to convince, Ixtl had oversold his case.

*   *   *   *   *

It was shortly after he had returned to Washington, that the aliens gave the waiting world the reasons for their appearance on Earth. They were, they said, members of a very ancient highly evolved culture called Aztlan. And the Aztlans, long past the need for conquest and expansion, had turned their mighty science to the help of other, less fortunate, races in the galaxy. The aliens were, in a sense, missionaries—one of hundreds of teams travelling the star lanes to bring the benefits of Aztlan culture to less favored worlds. They were, they unblushingly admitted, altruists—interested only in helping others.

It was pure corn, Matson reflected cynically, but the world lapped it up and howled for more. After decades of cold war, lukewarm war, and sporadic outbreaks of violence, that were inevitably building to atomic destruction, men were willing to try anything that would ease the continual burden of strain and worry. To Mankind, the Aztlans' words were as refreshing as a cool breeze of hope in a desert of despair.

And the world got what it wanted.

Quite suddenly the aliens left the Northwest, and accompanied by protective squads of FBI and Secret Service began to cross the nation. Taking widely separated paths they visited cities, towns, and farms, exhibiting the greatest curiosity about the workings of human civilization. And, in turn, they were examined by hordes of hopeful humans. Everywhere they went, they spread their message of good will and hope backed by the incredibly convincing power of their telepathic minds. Behind them, they left peace and hopeful calm; before them, anticipation mounted. It rose to a crescendo in New York where the paths of the star men met.

The Aztlans invaded the United Nations. They spoke to the General Assembly and the Security Council, were interviewed by the secretariat and reporters from a hundred foreign lands. They told their story with such conviction that even the Communist bloc failed to raise an objection, which was as amazing to the majority of the delegates as the fact of the star men themselves. Altruism, it seemed, had no conflict with dialectic materialism. The aliens offered a watered-down variety of their technology to the peoples of Earth with no strings attached, and the governments of Earth accepted with open hands, much as a small boy accepts a cookie from his mother. It was impossible for men to resist the lure of something for nothing, particularly when it was offered by such people as the Aztlans. After all, Matson reflected bitterly, nobody shoots Santa Claus!

From every nation in the world came invitations to the aliens to visit their lands. The star men cheerfully accepted. They moved across Europe, Asia, and Africa— visited South America, Central America, the Middle East and Oceania. No country escaped them. They absorbed languages, learned customs, and spread good will. Everywhere they went relaxation followed in their footsteps, and throughout the world arose a realization of the essential brotherhood of man.

It took nearly three years of continual travelling before the aliens again assembled at UN headquarters to begin the second part of their promised plan—to give their science to Earth. And men waited with calm expectation for the dawn of Golden Age.

Matson's lips twisted. Fools! Blind, stupid fools! Selling their birthright for a mess of pottage! He shifted the rifle across his knees and began filling the magazine with cartridges. He felt an empty loneliness as he closed the action over the filled magazine and turned the safety to "on". There was no comforting knowledge of support and sympathy to sustain him in what he was about to do. There was no real hope that there ever would be. His was a voice crying in the wilderness, a voice that was ignored—as it had been when he visited the President of the United States....

*   *   *   *   *

Matson entered the White House, presented his appointment card, and was ushered past ice-eyed Secret Service men into the presidential office. It was as close as he had ever been to the Chief Executive, and he stared with polite curiosity across the width of desk which separated them.

"I wanted to see you about the Aztlan business," the President began without preamble. "You were there when their ship landed, and you are also one of the few men in the country who has seen them alone. In addition, your office will probably be handling the bulk of our requests in regard to the offer they made yesterday in the UN. You're in a favorable spot." The President smiled and shrugged. "I wanted to talk with you sooner, but business and routine play the devil with one's desires in this office.

"Now tell me," he continued, "your impression of these people."

"They're an enigma," Matson said flatly. "To tell the truth, I can't figure them out." He ran his fingers through his hair with a worried gesture. "I'm supposed to be a pretty fair physicist, and I've had quite a bit of training in the social sciences, but both the mechanisms and the psychology of these Aztlans are beyond my comprehension. All I can say for sure is that they're as far beyond us as we are beyond the cavemen. In fact, we have so little in common that I can't think of a single reason why they would want to stay here, and the fact that they do only adds to my confusion."

"But you must have learned something," the President said.

"Oh we've managed to collect data," Matson replied. "But there's a lot of difference between data and knowledge."

"I can appreciate that, but I'd still like to know what you think. Your opinion could have some weight."

Matson doubted it. His opinions were contrary to those of the majority. Still, the Chief asked for it—and he might possibly have an open mind. It was a chance worth taking.

"Well, Sir, I suppose you've heard of the so-called "wild talents" some of our own people occasionally possess?"

The President nodded.

"It is my belief," Matson continued, "that the Aztlans possess these to a far greater degree than we do, and that their science is based upon them. They have something which they call psychomathematics, which by definition is the mathematics of the mind, and this seems to be the basis of their physical science. I saw their machines, and I must confess that their purpose baffled me until I realized that they must be mechanisms for amplifying their own natural equipment. We know little or nothing about psi phenomena, so it is no wonder I couldn't figure them out. As a matter of fact we've always treated psi as something that shouldn't be mentioned in polite scientific conversation."

The President grinned. "I always thought you boys had your blind spots."

"We do—but when we're confronted with a fact, we try to find out something about it—that is if the fact hits us hard enough, often enough."

"Well, you've been hit hard and often," the President chuckled, "What did you find out?"

"Facts," Matson said grimly, "just facts. Things that could be determined by observation and measurement. We know that the aliens are telepathic. We also know that they have a form of ESP—or perhaps a recognition of danger would be a better term—and we know its range is somewhat over a third of a mile. We know that they're telekinetic. The lack of visible controls in their ship would tell us that, even if we hadn't seen them move small objects at a distance. We know that they have eidetic memories, and that they can reason on an extremely high level. Other than that we know nothing. We don't even know their physical structure. We've tried X-ray but they're radio-opaque. We've tried using some human sensitives from the Rhine Institute, but they're unable to get anywhere. They just turn empathic in the aliens' presence, and when we get them back, they do nothing but babble about the beauty of the Aztlan soul."

"Considering the difficulties, you haven't done too badly," the President said. "I take it then, that you're convinced that they are an advanced life form. But do you think they're sincere in their attitude toward us?"

"Oh, they're sincere enough," Matson said. "The only trouble is that we don't know just what they're sincere about. You see, sir, we are in the position of a savage to whom a trader brings the luxuries of civilization. To the savage, the trader may represent purest altruism, giving away such valuable things as glass beads and machine made cloth for useless pieces of yellow rock and the skins of some native pest. The savage hasn't the slightest inkling that he's being exploited. By the time he realizes he's been had, and the yellow rock is gold and the skins are mink, he has become so dependent upon the goods for which the trader has whetted his appetite that he inevitably becomes an economic slave.

"Of course you can argue that the cloth and beads are far more valuable to the savage than the gold or mink.

But in the last analysis, value is determined by the higher culture, and by that standard, the savage gets taken. And ultimately civilization moves in and the superior culture of the trader's race determines how the savage will act.

"Still, the savage has a basis for his acts. He is giving something for something—making a trade. But we're not even in that position. The aliens apparently want nothing from us. They have asked for nothing except our good will, and that isn't a tradable item."

"But they're altruists!" the President protested.

"Sir, do you think that they're insane?" Matson asked curiously. "Do they appear like fanatics to you?"

"But we can't apply our standards to them. You yourself have said that their civilization is more advanced than ours."

"Whose standards can we apply?" Matson asked. "If not ours, then whose? The only standards that we can possibly apply are our own, and in the entire history of human experience there has never been a single culture that has had a basis of pure altruism. Such a culture could not possibly exist. It would be overrun and gobbled up by its practical neighbors before it drew its first breath.

"We must assume that the culture from which these aliens come has had a practical basis in its evolutionary history. It could not have risen full blown and altruistic like Minerva from the brain of Jove. And if the culture had a practical basis in the past, it logically follows that it has a practical basis in the present. Such a survival trait as practicality would probably never be lost no matter how far the Aztlan race has evolved. Therefore, we must concede that they are practical people—people who do not give away something for nothing. But the question still remains—what do they want?

"Whatever it is, I don't think it is anything from which we will profit. No matter how good it looks, I am convinced that cooperation with these aliens will not ultimately be to our advantage. Despite the reports of every investigative agency in this government, I cannot believe that any such thing as pure altruism exists in a sane mind. And whatever I may believe about the Aztlans, I do not think they're insane."

The President sighed. "You are a suspicious man, Matson, and perhaps you are right; but it doesn't matter what you believe—or what I believe for that matter. This government has decided to accept the help the Aztlans are so graciously offering. And until the reverse is proven, we must accept the fact that the star men *are* altruists, and work with them on that basis. You will organize your office along those lines, and extract every gram of information that you can. Even you must admit that they have knowledge that will improve our American way of life."

Matson shook his head doggedly. "I'm afraid, Sir, if you expect Aztlan science to improve the American way of life, you are going to be disappointed. It might promote an Aztlan way of life, but the reverse is hardly possible."

"It's not my decision," the President said. "My hands are tied. Congress voted for the deal by acclamation early this morning. I couldn't veto it even if I wanted to."

"I cannot cooperate in what I believe is our destruction." Matson said in a flat voice.

"Then you have only one course," the President said. "I will be forced to accept your resignation." He sighed wearily.

"Personally, I think you're making a mistake. Think it over before you decide. You're a good man, and Lord knows the government can use good men. There are far too many fools in politics." He shrugged and stood up. The interview was over.

Matson returned to his offices, filled with cold frustration. Even the President believed he could do nothing, and these shortsighted politicians who could see nothing more than the immediate gains—there was a special hell reserved for them. There were too many fools in politics. However, he would do what he could. His sense of duty was stronger than his resentment. He would stay on and try to cushion some of the damage which the Aztlans would inevitably cause, no matter how innocent their motives. And perhaps the President was right—perhaps the alien science would bring more good than harm.

*   *   *   *   *

For the next two years Matson watched the spread of Aztlan ideas throughout the world. He saw Aztlan devices bring health, food and shelter to millions in underprivileged countries, and improve the lot of those in more favored nations. He watched tyrannies and authoritarian governments fall under the passive resistance of their peoples. He saw militarism crumble to impotence as the Aztlan influence spread through every facet of society, first as a trickle, then as a steady stream, and finally as a rushing torrent. He saw Mankind on the brink of a Golden Age—and he was unsatisfied.

Reason said that the star men were exactly what they claimed to be. Their every action proved it. Their consistency was perfect, their motives unimpeachable, and the results of their efforts were astounding. Life on Earth was becoming pleasant for millions who never knew the meaning of the word. Living standards improved, and everywhere men were conscious of a feeling of warmth and brotherhood. There was no question that the aliens were doing exactly what they promised.

But reason also told him that the aliens were subtly and methodically destroying everything that man had created, turning him from an individual into a satisfied puppet operated by Aztlan strings. For man is essentially lazy—always searching for the easier way. Why should he struggle to find an answer when the Aztlans had discovered it millennia ago and were perfectly willing to share their knowledge? Why should he use inept human devices when those of the aliens performed similar operations with infinitely more ease and efficiency? Why should he work when all he had to do was ask? There was plan behind their acts.

But at that point reason dissolved into pure speculation. Why were they doing this? Was it merely mistaken kindliness or was there a deeper more subtle motive? Matson didn't know, and in that lack of knowledge lay the hell in which he struggled.

For two years he stayed on with the OSR, watching humanity rush down an unmarked road to an uncertain future. Then he ran away. He could take no more of this blind dependence upon alien wisdom. And with the change in administration that had occurred in the fall elections he no longer had the sense of personal loyalty to the President which had kept him working at a job he despised. He wanted no part of this brave new world the aliens were creating. He wanted to be alone. Like a hermit of ancient times who abandoned society to seek his soul, Matson fled to the desert country of the Southwest—as far as possible from the Aztlans and their works.

The grimly beautiful land toughened his muscles, blackened his skin, and brought him a measure of peace. Humanity retreated to remoteness except for Seth Winters, a leathery old-timer he had met on his first trip into the desert. The acquaintance had ripened to friendship. Seth furnished a knowledge of the desert country which Matson lacked, and Matson's money provided the occasional grubstake they needed. For weeks at a time they never saw another human—and Matson was satisfied. The world could go its own way. He would go his.

Running away was the smartest thing he could have done. Others more brave perhaps, or perhaps less rational—had tried to fight, to form an underground movement to oppose these altruists from space; but they were a tiny minority so divided in motives and purpose that they could not act as a unit. They were never more than a nuisance, and without popular support they never had a chance. After the failure of a complicated plot to assassinate the aliens, they were quickly rounded up and confined. And the aliens continued their work.

Matson shrugged. It was funny how little things could mark mileposts in a man's life. If he had known of the underground he probably would have joined it and suffered the same penalty for failure. If he hadn't fled, if he hadn't met Seth Winters, if he hadn't taken that last trip into the desert, if any one of a hundred little things had happened differently he would not be here. That last trip into the desert—he remembered it as though it were yesterday....

The yellow flare of a greasewood fire cast flickering spears of light into the encircling darkness. Above, in the purplish black vault of the moonless sky the stars shone down with icy splendor. The air was quiet, the evening breeze had died, and the stillness of the desert night pressed softly upon the earth. Far away, muted by distance, came the ululating wail of a coyote.

Seth Winters laid another stick of quick-burning greasewood on the fire and squinted across the smoke at Matson who was lying on his back, arms crossed behind his head, eyeing the night sky with the fascination of a dreamer.

"It's certainly peaceful out here," Matson murmured as he rose to his feet, stretched, and sat down again looking into the tiny fire.

"'Tain't nothin' unusual, Dan'l. Not out here it ain't. It's been plumb peaceful on this here desert nigh onto a million years. An' why's it peaceful? Mainly 'cuz there ain't too many humans messin' around in it."

"Possibly you're right, Seth."

"Shore I'm right. It jest ain't nacheral fer a bunch of Homo saps to get together without an argyment startin' somewhere. 'Tain't the nature of the critter to be peaceable. An' y'know, thet's the part of this here sweetness an' light between nations that bothers me. Last time I was in Prescott, I set down an' read six months of newspapers—an' everything's jest too damn good to be true. Seems like everybody's gettin' to love everybody else." He shook his head. "The hull world's as sticky-sweet as molasses candy. It jest ain't nacheral!"

"The star men are keeping their word. They said that they would bring us peace. Isn't that what they're doing?"

"Shucks Dan'l—that don't give 'em no call to make the world a blasted honey-pot with everybody bubblin' over with brotherly love. There ain't no real excitement left. Even the Commies ain't raisin' hell like they useta. People are gettin' more like a bunch of damn woolies every day."

"I'll admit that Mankind had herd instincts," Matson replied lazily, "but I've never thought of them as particularly sheeplike. More like a wolf pack, I'd say."

"Wal, there's nothin' wolflike about 'em right now. Look, Dan'l, yuh know what a wolf pack's like. They're smart, tough, and mean—an' the old boss wolf is the smartest, toughest, and meanest critter in the hull pack. The others respect him 'cuz he's proved his ability to lead. But take a sheep flock now—the bellwether is jest a nice gentle old castrate thet'll do jest whut the sheepherder wants. He's got no originality. He's jest a noise thet the rest foller."

"Could be."

"It shore is! Jes f'r instance, an' speakin' of bellwethers, have yuh ever heard of a character called Throckmorton Bixbee?"

"Can't say I have. He sounds like a nance."

"Whutever a nance is—he's it! But yuh're talkin' about our next President, unless all the prophets are wrong. He's jest as bad as his name. Of all the gutless wonders I've ever heard of that pilgrim takes the prize. He even looks like a rabbit!"

"I can see where I had better catch up on some contemporary history," Matson said. "I've been out in the sticks too long."

"If yuh know what's good fer yuh, yuh'll stay here. The rest of the country's goin' t'hell. Brother Bixbee's jest a sample. About the only thing that'd recommend him is that he's hot fer peace—an' he's got those furriners' blessing. Seems like those freaks swing a lotta weight nowadays, an' they ain't shy about tellin' folks who an' what they favor. They've got bold as brass this past year."

Matson nodded idly—then stiffened—turning a wide eyed stare on Seth. A blinding light exploded in his brain as the words sank in. With crystal clarity he knew the answer! He laughed harshly.

Winters stared at him with mild surprise. "What's bit yuh, Dan'l?"

But Matson was completely oblivious, busily buttressing the flash of inspiration. Sure—that was the only thing it could be! Those aliens were working on a program—one that was grimly recognizable once his attention was focussed on it. There must have been considerable pressure to make them move so fast that a short-lived human could see what they were planning— but Matson had a good idea of what was driving them, an atomic war that could decimate the world would be all the spur they'd need!

They weren't playing for penny ante stakes. They didn't want to exploit Mankind. They didn't give a damn about Mankind! To them humanity was merely an unavoidable nuisance—something to be pushed aside, to be made harmless and dependent, and ultimately to be quietly and bloodlessly eliminated. Man's civilization held nothing that the star men wanted, but man's planet— that was a different story! Truly the aliens were right when they considered man a savage. Like the savage, man didn't realize his most valuable possession was his land!

The peaceful penetration was what had fooled him. Mankind, faced with a similar situation, and working from a position of overwhelming strength would have reacted differently. Humanity would have invaded and conquered. But the aliens had not even considered this obvious step.

Why?

The answer was simple and logical. They couldn't! Even though their technology was advanced enough to exterminate man with little or no loss to themselves, combat and slaughter must be repulsive to them. It had to be. With their telepathic minds they would necessarily have a pathologic horror of suffering. They were so highly evolved that they simply couldn't fight—at least not with the weapons of humanity. But they could use the subtler weapon of altruism!

And even more important—uncontrolled emotions were poison to them. In fact Ixtl had admitted it back in Seattle. The primitive psi waves of humanity's hates, lusts, fears, and exultations must be unbearable torture to a race long past such animal outbursts. That was—must be—why they were moving so fast. For their own safety, emotion had to be damped out of the human race.

Matson had a faint conception of what the aliens must have suffered when they first surveyed that crowd at International Airport. No wonder they looked so strangely immobile at that first contact! The raw emotion must have nearly killed them! He felt a reluctant stir of admiration for their courage, for the dedicated bravery needed to face that crowd and establish a beachhead of tranquility. Those first few minutes must have had compressed in them the agonies of a lifetime!

Matson grinned coldly. The aliens were not invulnerable. If Mankind could be taught to fear and hate them, and if that emotion could be focussed, they never again would try to take this world. It would be sheer suicide. As long as Mankind kept its emotions it would be safe from this sort of invasion. But the problem was to teach Mankind to fear and hate. Shock would do it, but how could that shock be applied?

The thought led inevitably to the only possible conclusion. The aliens would have to be killed, and in such a manner as to make humanity fear retaliation from the stars. Fear would unite men against a possible invasion, and fear would force men to reach for the stars to forestall retribution.

Matson grinned thinly. Human nature couldn't have changed much these past years. Even with master psychologists like the Aztlans operating upon it, changes in emotional pattern would require generations. He sighed, looked into the anxious face of Seth Winters, and returned to the reality of the desert night. His course was set. He knew what he had to do.

*   *   *   *   *

He laid the rifle across his knees and opened the little leather box sewn to the side of the guncase. With precise, careful movements he removed the silencer and fitted it to the threaded muzzle of the gun. The bulky, blue excrescence changed the rifle from a thing of beauty to one of murder. He looked at it distastefully, then shrugged and stretched out on the mattress, easing the ugly muzzle through the hole in the brickwork. It wouldn't be long now....

He glanced upward through the window above him at the Weather Bureau instruments atop a nearby building. The metal cups of the anemometer hung motionless against the metallic blue of the sky. No wind stirred in the deep canyons of the city streets as the sun climbed in blazing splendor above the towering buildings. He moved a trifle, shifting the muzzle of the gun until it bore upon the sidewalks. The telescopic sight picked out faces from the waiting crowd with a crystal clarity. Everywhere was the same sheeplike placidity. He shuddered, the sights jumping crazily from one face to another,—wondering if he had misjudged his race, if he had really come too late, if he had underestimated the powers of the Aztlans.

Far down the avenue, an excited hum came to his ears, and the watching crowd stirred. Faces lighted and Matson sighed. He was not wrong. Emotion was only suppressed, not vanished. There was still time!

The aliens were coming. Coming to cap the climax of their pioneer work, to drive the first nail in humanity's coffin! For the first time in history man's dream of the brotherhood of man was close to reality.

And he was about to destroy it! The irony bit into Matson's soul, and for a moment he hesitated, feeling the wave of tolerance and good will rising from the street below. Did he have the right to destroy man's dream? Did he dare tamper with the will of the world? Had he the right to play God?

The parade came slowly down the happy street, a kaleidoscope of color and movement that approached and went past in successive waves and masses. This was a gala day, this eve of world union! The insigne of the UN was everywhere. The aliens had used the organization to further their plans and it was now all-powerful. A solid bank of UN flags led the van of delegates, smiling and swathed in formal dress, sitting erect in their black official cars draped with the flags of native lands that would soon be furled forever if the aliens had their way.

And behind them came the Aztlans!

They rode together, standing on a pure white float, a bar of dazzling white in a sea of color. All equal, their inhumanly beautiful faces calm and remote, the Aztlans rode through the joyful crowd. There was something inspiring about the sight and for a moment, Matson felt a wave of revulsion sweep through him.

He sighed and thumbed the safety to "off", pulled the cocking lever and slid the first cartridge into the breech. He settled himself drawing a breath of air into his lungs, letting a little dribble out through slack lips, catching the remainder of the exhalation with closed glottis. The sights wavered and steadied upon the head of the center alien, framing the pale noble face with its aureole of golden hair. The luminous eyes were dull and introspective as the alien tried to withdraw from the emotions of the crowd. There was no awareness of danger on the alien's face. At 600 yards he was beyond their esper range and he was further covered by the feelings of the crowd. The sights lowered to the broad chest and centered there as Matson's spatulate fingers took up the slack in the trigger and squeezed softly and steadily.

A coruscating glow bathed the bodies of three of the aliens as their tall forms jerked to the smashing impact of the bullets! Their metallic tunics melted and sloughed as inner fires ate away the fragile garments that covered them! Flexible synthetic skin cracked and curled in the infernal heat, revealing padding, wirelike tendons, rope-like cords of flexible tubing and a metallic skeleton that melted and dripped in white hot drops in the heat of atomic flame—

"Robots!" Matson gasped with sudden blinding realization. "I should have known! No wonder they seemed inhuman. Their builders would never dare expose themselves to the furies and conflicts of our emotionally uncontrolled world!"

One of the aliens crouched on the float, his four-fingered hands pressed against a smoking hole in his metal tunic. The smoke thickened and a yellowish ichor poured out bursting into flame on contact with the air. The fifth alien, Ixtl, was untouched, standing with hands widestretched in a gesture that at once held command and appeal.

Matson reloaded quickly, but held his fire. The swarming crowd surrounding the alien was too thick for a clear shot and Matson, with sudden revulsion, was unwilling to risk further murder in a cause already won. The tall, silver figure of the alien winced and shuddered, his huge body shaking like a leaf in a storm! His builders had never designed him to withstand the barrage of focused emotion that was sweeping from the crowd. Terror, shock, sympathy, hate, loathing, grief, and disillusionment—the incredible gamut of human feelings wrenched and tore at the Aztlan, shorting delicate circuits, ripping the poised balance of his being as the violent discordant blasts lanced through him with destroying energy! Ixtl's classic features twisted in a spasm of inconceivable agony, a thin curl of smoke drifted from his distorted tragic mask of a mouth as he crumpled, a pitiful deflated figure against the whiteness of the float.

The cries of fear and horror changed their note as the aliens' true nature dawned upon the crowd. Pride of flesh recoiled as the swarming humans realized the facts. Revulsion at being led by machines swelled into raw red rage. The mob madness spread as an ominous growl began rising from the streets.

A panicky policeman triggered it, firing his Aztlan-built shock tube into the forefront of the mob. A dozen men fell, to be trampled by their neighbors as a swarm of men and women poured over the struggling officer and buried him from sight. Like wildfire, pent-up emotions blazed out in a flame of fury. The parade vanished, sucked into the maelstrom and torn apart. Fists flew, flesh tore, men and women screamed in high bitter agony as the mob clawed and trampled in a surging press of writhing forms that filled the street from one line of buildings to the other.

Half-mad with triumph, drunk with victory, shocked at the terrible form that death had taken in coming to Ixtl, Matson raised his clenched hands to the sky and screamed in a raw inhuman voice, a cry in which all of man's violence and pride were blended! The spasm passed as quickly as it came, and with its passing came exhaustion. The job was done. The aliens were destroyed. Tomorrow would bring reaction and with it would come fear.

Tomorrow or the next day man would hammer out a true world union, spurred by the thought of a retribution that would never come. Yet all that didn't matter. The important thing—the only important thing—was preserved. Mankind would have to unite for survival—or so men would think—and he would never disillusion them. For this was man's world, and men were again free to work out their own destiny for better or for worse, without interference, and without help. The golden dream was over. Man might fail, but if he did he would fail on his own terms. And if he succeeded—Matson looked up grimly at the shining sky....

Slowly he rose to his feet and descended to the raging street below.

INSIDEKICK

ILLUSTRATED BY WOOD
ORIGINALLY PUBLISHED IN *GALAXY SCIENCE FICTION*,
FEBRUARY 1959

Johnson had two secrets—
one he knew and would die rather than reveal—
and one he didn't know that meant to save him over
his own dead body!

INSIDEKICK

The rifle lay comfortably in his hands, a gleaming precision instrument that exuded a faint odor of gun oil and powder solvent. It was a perfect specimen of the gunsmith's art, a semi-automatic rifle with a telescopic sight—a precisely engineered tool that could hurl death with pinpoint accuracy for better than half a mile. Shifaz glanced furtively around the room. Satisfied that it was empty except for Fred Kemmer and himself, he sidled up to the Earthman's desk and hissed conspiratorially in his ear, "Sir, this Johnson is a spy! Is it permitted to slay him?"

"It is permitted," Kemmer said in a tone suitable to the gravity of the occasion.

He watched humorlessly as the Antarian slithered out of the office with a flutter of colorful ceremonial robes. Both Kemmer and Shifaz had known for weeks that Johnson was a spy, but the native had to go through this insane rigmarole before the rules on Antar would allow him to act. At any rate, the formalities were over at last and the affair should be satisfactorily ended before nightfall. Natives moved quickly enough, once the preliminaries were concluded.

Kemmer leaned back in his chair and sighed. Being the Interworld Corporation's local manager had more compensations than headaches, despite the rigid ritualism of native society. Since most of the local population was under his thumb, counter-espionage was miraculously effective. This fellow Johnson, for instance, had been in Vaornia less than three weeks, and despite the fact that he was an efficient and effective snoop, he had been fingered less than forty-eight hours after his arrival in the city.

Kemmer closed his eyes and let a smile cross his keen features. Under his administration, there would be a sharp rise in the mortality curve for spies detected in the Vaornia-Lagash-Timargh triangle. With the native judiciary firmly under IC control, the Corporation literally had a free hand, providing it kept its nose superficially clean. And as for spies, they knew the chances they took and what the penalty could be for interfering with the normal operations of corporate business.

Kemmer yawned, stretched, turned his attention to more important matters.

*   *   *   *   *

Albert Johnson fumbled hopefully in the empty food container before tossing it aside. A plump, prosaic man of middle height, with a round ingenuous face, Albert was as undistinguished as his name, a fact that made him an excellent investigator. But he was neither undistinguished nor unnoticed in his present position, although he had tried to carry it off by photographing the actions of the local Sanitary Processional like any tourist.

He had been waiting near the Vaornia Arm on the road that led to Lagash since early afternoon, and now it was nearly evening. He cursed mildly at the fact that the natives had no conception of time, a trait not exclusively Antarian, but one which was developed to a high degree on this benighted planet. And the fact that he was hungry didn't add to his good temper. Natives might be able to fast for a week without ill effects, but his chunky body demanded quantities of nourishment at regular intervals, and his stomach was protesting audibly at being empty.

He looked around him, at the rutted road, and at the darkening Vaornia Arm of the Devan Forest that bordered the roadway. The Sanitary Processional had completed the daily ritual of waste disposal and the cart drivers and censer bearers were goading their patient daks into a faster gait. It wasn't healthy to be too near the forest after the sun went down. The night beasts weren't particular about what, or whom, they ate.

The Vaornese used the Vaornia Arm as a dump for the refuse of the city, a purpose admirably apt, for the ever-hungry forest life seldom left anything uneaten by morning. And since Antarian towns had elaborate rituals concerning the disposal of waste, together with a nonexistent sewage system, the native attitude of fatalistic indifference to an occasional tourist or Antarian being gobbled up by some nightmare denizen of the forest was understandable.

The fact that the Arm was also an excellent place to dispose of an inconvenient body didn't occur to Albert until the three natives with knives detached themselves from the rear of the Sanitary Processional and advanced upon him. They came from three directions, effectively boxing him in, and Albert realized with a sick certainty that he had been double-crossed, that Shifaz, instead of being an informant for him, was working for the IC. Albert turned to face the nearest native, tensing his muscles for battle.

Then he saw the Zark.

It stepped out of the gathering darkness of the forest, and with its appearance everything stopped. For perhaps a micro-second, the three Vaornese stood frozen. Then, with a simultaneous wheep of terror, they turned and ran for the city.

They might have stayed and finished their work if they had known it was a Zark, but at the moment the Zark was energizing a toothy horror that Earthmen called a Bandersnatch—an insane combination of talons, teeth and snakelike neck mounted on a crocodilian body that exuded an odor of putrefaction from the carrion upon which it normally fed. The Bandersnatch had been dead for several hours, but neither the natives nor Albert knew that.

*   *   *   *   *

It was a tribute to the Zark's ability to maintain pseudo-life in a Bandersnatch carcass that the knifemen fled and a similar panic seized the late travelers on the road. Albert stared with horrified fascination at the monstrosity for several seconds before he, too, fled. Any number of natives with knives were preferable to a Bandersnatch. He had hesitated only because he didn't possess the conditioned reflexes arising from generations of exposure to Antarian wildlife.

He was some twenty yards behind the rearmost native, and, though not designed for speed, was actually gaining upon the fellow, when his foot struck a loose cobblestone in the road. Arms flailing, legs pumping desperately to balance his toppling mass, Albert fought manfully against the forces of gravity and inertia.

He lost.

His head struck another upturned cobble. His body twitched once and then relaxed limply and unconscious upon the dusty road.

The Zark winced a little at the sight, certain that this curious creature had damaged itself seriously.

Filled with compassion, it started forward on the Bandersnatch's four walking legs, the grasping talons crossed on the breast in an attitude of prayer. The Zark wasn't certain what it could do, but perhaps it could help.

Albert was mercifully unconscious as it bent over him to inspect his prone body with a purple-lidded pineal eye that was blue with concern. The Zark noted the bruise upon his forehead and marked his regular breathing, and came to the correct conclusion that, whatever had happened, the biped was relatively undamaged. But the Zark didn't go away. It had never seen a human in its thousand-odd years of existence, which was not surprising since Earthmen had been on Antar less than a decade and Zarks seldom left the forest.

Albert began to stir before the Zark remembered its present condition. Not being a carnivore, it saw nothing appetizing about Albert, but it was energizing a Bandersnatch, and, like all Zarks, it was a purist. A living Bandersnatch would undoubtedly drool happily at the sight of such a tempting tidbit, so the Zark opened the three-foot jaws and drooled.

Albert chose this precise time to return to consciousness. He turned his head groggily and looked up into a double row of saw-edged teeth surmounted by a leering triangle of eyes. A drop of viscid drool splattered moistly on his forehead, and as the awful face above him bent closer to his own, he fainted.

The Zark snapped its jaws disapprovingly. This was not the proper attitude to take in the presence of a ferocious monster. One simply didn't go to sleep. One should attempt to run. The biped's act was utterly illogical. It needed investigation.

*　　*　　*　　*　　*

Curiously, the Zark sent out a pseudopod of its substance through the open mouth of its disguise. The faintly glittering thread oozed downward and struck Albert's head beside his right eye. Without pausing, the thread sank through skin and connective tissue, circled the eyeball and located the optic nerve. It raced inward along the nerve trunk, split at the optic chiasma, and entered the corpora quadrigemina where it branched into innumerable microscopic filaments that followed the main neural paths of the man's brain, probing the major areas of thought and reflex.

The Zark quivered with pleasure. The creature was beautifully complex, and, more important, untenanted. He would make an interesting host.

The Zark didn't hesitate. It needed a host; giving its present mass of organic matter pseudo-life took too much energy. The Bandersnatch collapsed with a faint slurping sound. A blob of iridescent jelly flowed from the mouth and spread itself evenly over Albert's body in a thin layer. The jelly shimmered, glowed, disappeared inward through Albert's clothing and skin, diffusing through the subcutaneous tissues, sending hair-like threads along nerve trunks and blood vessels until the threads met other threads and joined, and the Zark became a network of protoplasmic tendrils that ramified through Albert's body.

Immediately the Zark turned its attention to the task of adapting itself to its new host. Long ago it had learned that this had to be done quickly or the host did not survive. And since the tissues of this new host were considerably different from those of the Bandersnatch, a great number of structural and chemical changes had to be made quickly. With some dismay, the Zark realized that its own stores of energy would be insufficient for the task. It would have to borrow energy from the host— which was a poor way to start a symbiotic relationship. Ordinarily, one gave before taking.

Fortunately, Albert possessed considerable excess fat, an excellent source of energy whose removal would do no harm. There was plenty here for both Albert and itself. The man's body twitched and jerked as the Zark's protean cells passed through the adaptive process, and as the last leukocyte recoiled from tissue that had suddenly become normal, his consciousness returned. Less than ten minutes had passed, but they were enough. The Zark was safely in harmony with its new host.

Albert opened his eyes and looked wildly around. The landscape was empty of animate life except for the odorous carcass of the Bandersnatch lying beside him. Albert shivered, rose unsteadily to his feet and began walking toward Vaornia. That he didn't run was only because he couldn't.

He found it hard to believe that he was still alive. Yet a hurried inspection convinced him that there wasn't a tooth mark on him. It was a miracle that left him feeling vaguely uneasy. He wished he knew what had killed that grinning horror so opportunely. But then, on second thought, maybe it was better that he didn't know. There might be things in the Devan Forest worse than a Bandersnatch.

* * * * *

Inside the city walls, Vaornia struck a three-pronged blow at Albert's senses. Sight, hearing and smell were assaulted simultaneously. Natives slithered past, garbed in long robes of garish color. Sibilant voices cut through the evening air like thin-edged knives clashing against the grating screech of the ungreased wooden wheels of dak carts. Odors of smoke, cooking, spices, perfume and corruption mingled with the all-pervasive musky stench of unwashed Vaornese bodies.

It was old to Albert, but new and exciting to the Zark. Its taps on Albert's sense organs brought a flood of new sensation the Zark had never experienced. It marveled at the crowded buildings studded with jutting balconies and ornamental carvings. It stared at the dak caravans maneuvering with ponderous delicacy through the swarming crowds. It reveled in the colorful banners and awnings of the tiny shops lining the streets, and the fluttering robes of the natives. Color was something new to the Zark. Its previous hosts had been color blind, and the symbiont wallowed in an orgy of bright sensation.

If Albert could have tuned in on his fellow traveler's emotions, he probably would have laughed. For the Zark was behaving precisely like the rubbernecking tourist he himself was pretending to be. But Albert wasn't interested in the sights, sounds or smells, nor did the natives intrigue him. There was only one of them he cared to meet—that slimy doublecrosser called Shifaz who had nearly conned him into a one-way ticket.

Albert plowed heedlessly through the crowd, using his superior mass to remove natives from his path. By completely disregarding the code of conduct outlined by the IC travel bureau, he managed to make respectable progress toward the enormous covered area in the center of town that housed the Kazlak, or native marketplace. Shifaz had a stand there where he was employed as a tourist guide.

The Zark, meanwhile, was not idle despite the outside interests. The majority of its structure was busily engaged in checking and cataloguing the body of its host, an automatic process that didn't interfere with the purely intellectual one of enjoying the new sensations. Albert's body wasn't in too bad shape. A certain amount of repair work would have to be done, but despite the heavy padding of fat, the organs were in good working condition.

The Zark ruminated briefly over what actions it should take as it dissolved a milligram of cholesterol out of Albert's aorta and strengthened the weak spot in the blood vessel with a few cells of its own substance until Albert's tissues could fill the gap. Its knowledge of human physiology was incomplete, but it instinctively recognized abnormality. As a result, it could help the host's physical condition, which was a distinct satisfaction, for a Zark must be helpful.

*   *   *   *   *

Shifaz was at his regular stand, practicing his normal profession of guide. As Albert approached, he was in the midst of describing the attractions of the number two tour to a small knot of fascinated tourists.

"And then, in the center of the Kazlak, we will come to the Hall of the Brides—Antar's greatest marriage market. It has been arranged for you to actually see a mating auction in progress, but we must hurry or—" Shifaz looked up to see Albert shouldering the tourists aside. His yellow eyes widened and his hand darted to his girdle and came up with a knife.

The nearest tourists fell back in alarm as he hissed malevolently at Albert, "Stand back, Earthman, or I'll let the life out of your scaleless carcass!"

"Doublecrosser," Albert said, moving in. One meaty hand closed over the knife hand and wrenched while the other caught Shifaz alongside the head with a smack that sounded loud in the sudden quiet. Shifaz did a neat backflip and lay prostrate, the tip of his tail twitching reflexively.

One of the tourists screamed.

"No show today, folks," Albert said. "Shifaz has another engagement." He picked the Antarian up by a fold of his robe and shook him like a dirty dustcloth. A number of items cascaded out of hidden pockets, among which was an oiled-silk pouch. Albert dropped the native and picked up the pouch, opened it, sniffed, and nodded.

It fitted. Things were clearer now.

He was still nodding when two Earthmen in IC uniform stepped out of the crowd. "Sorry, sir," the bigger of the pair said, "but you have just committed a violation of the IC-Antar Compact. I'm afraid we'll have to take you in."

"This lizard tried to have me killed," Albert protested.

"I wouldn't know about that," the IC man said. "You've assaulted a native, and that's a crime. You'd better come peaceably with us—local justice is rather primitive and unpleasant."

"I'm an Earth citizen—" Albert began.

"This world is on a commercial treaty." The guard produced a blackjack and tapped the shot-filled leather in his palm. "It's our business to protect people like you from the natives, and if you insist, we'll use force."

"I don't insist, but I think you're being pretty high-handed."

"Your objection has been noted," the IC man said, "and will be included in the official report. Now come along or we'll be in the middle of a jurisdictional hassle when the native cops arrive. The corporation doesn't like hassles. They're bad for business."

*   *   *   *   *

The two IC men herded him into a waiting ground car and drove away. It was all done very smoothly, quietly and efficiently. The guards were good.

And so was the local detention room. It was clean, modern and—Albert noted wryly—virtually escape-proof. Albert was something of an expert on jails, and the thick steel bars, the force lock, and the spy cell in the ceiling won his grudging respect.

He sighed and sat down on the cot which was the room's sole article of furniture. He had been a fool to let his anger get the better of him. IC would probably use this brush with Shifaz as an excuse to send him back to Earth as an undesirable tourist—which would be the end of his mission here, and a black mark on a singularly unspotted record.

Of course, they might not be so gentle with him if they knew that he knew they were growing tobacco. But he didn't think that they would know—and if they had checked his background, they would find that he was an investigator for the Revenue Service. Technically, criminal operations were not his affair. His field was tax evasion.

He didn't worry too much about the fact that Shifaz had tried to kill him. On primitive worlds like this, that was a standard procedure—it was less expensive to kill an agent than bribe him or pay honest taxes. He was angry with himself for allowing the native to trick him.

He shrugged. By all rules of the game, IC would now admit about a two per cent profit on their Antar operation rather than the four per cent loss they had claimed, and pay up like gentlemen—and he would get skinned by the Chief back at Earth Central for allowing IC to unmask him. His report on tobacco growing would be investigated, but with the sketchy information he possessed, his charges would be impossible to prove—and IC would have plenty of time to bury the evidence.

If Earth Central hadn't figured that the corporation owed it some billion megacredits in back taxes, he wouldn't be here. He had been dragged from his job in the General Accounting Office, for every field man and ex-field man was needed to conduct the sweeping investigation. Every facet of the sprawling IC operation was being checked. Even minor and out-of-the-way spots like Antar were on the list—spots that normally demanded a cursory once-over by a second-class business technician.

*   *   *   *   *

Superficially, Antar had the dull unimportance of an early penetration. There were the usual trading posts, pilot plants, wholesale and retail trade, and tourist and recreation centers—all designed to accustom the native inhabitants to the presence of Earthmen and their works—and set them up for the commercial kill, after they had acquired a taste for the products of civilization. But although the total manpower and physical plant for a world of this size was right, its distribution was wrong.

A technician probably wouldn't see it, but to an agent who had dealt with corporate operations for nearly a quarter of a century, the setup felt wrong. It was not designed for maximum return. The Vaornia-Lagash-

Timargh triangle held even more men and material then Prime Base. That didn't make sense. It was inefficient, and IC was not noted for inefficiency.

Not being oriented criminally, Albert found out IC's real reason for concentration in this area only by absent-mindedly lighting a cigarette one day in Vaornia. He had realized almost instantly that this was a gross breach of outworld ethics and had thrown the cigarette away. It landed between a pair of Vaornese walking by.

The two goggled at the cigarette, sniffed the smoke rising from it, and with simultaneous whistles of surprise bent over to pick it up. Their heads collided with some force. The cigarette tore in their greedy grasp as they hissed hatefully at each other for a moment, before turning hostile glares in his direction. From their expressions, they thought this was a low Earthie trick to rob them of their dignity. Then they stalked off, their neck scales ruffled in anger, shreds of the cigarette still clutched in their hands.

Even Albert couldn't miss the implications. His tossing the butt away had produced the same reaction as a deck of morphine on a group of human addicts. Since IC wouldn't corrupt a susceptible race with tobacco when there were much cheaper legal ways, the logical answer was that it wasn't expensive on this planet—which argued that Antar was being set up for plantation operations—in which case tobacco addiction was a necessary prerequisite and the concentration of IC population made sense.

Now tobacco, as any Earthman knew, was the only monopoly in the Confederation, and Earth had maintained that monopoly by treaty and by force, despite numerous efforts to break it. There were some good reasons for the policy, ranging all the way from vice control to taxable income, but the latter was by far the most important. The revenue supported a considerable section of Earth Central as well as the huge battle fleet that maintained peace and order along the spacelanes and between the worlds.

But a light-weight, high-profit item like tobacco was a constant temptation to any sharp operator who cared more for money than for law, and IC filled that definition perfectly. In the Tax Section's book, the Interworld Corporation was a corner-cutting, profit-grabbing chiseler. Its basic character had been the same for three centuries, despite all the complete turnovers in staff. Albert grinned wryly. The old-timers were right when they made corporations legal persons.

Cigarettes which cost five credits to produce and sold for as high as two hundred would always interest a crook, and, as a consequence, Earth Central was always investigating reports of illegal plantations. They were found and destroyed eventually, and the owners punished. But the catch lay in the word "eventually." And if the operator was a corporation, no regulatory agency in its right mind would dare apply the full punitive power of the law. In that direction lay political suicide, for nearly half the population of Earth got dividends or salaries from them.

That, of course, was the trouble with corporations. They invariably grew too big and too powerful. But to break them up as the Ancients did was to destroy their efficiency. What was really needed was a corporate conscience.

Albert chuckled. That was a nice unproductive thought.

*   *   *   *   *

Fred Kemmer received the news that Albert had been taken to detention with a philosophic calm that lasted for nearly half an hour. By morning, the man would be turned over to the Patrol in Prime Base. The Patrol would support the charge that Albert was an undesirable tourist and send him home to Earth.

But the philosophic calm departed with a frantic leap when Shifaz reported Johnson's inspection of the oiled-silk pouch. Raw tobacco was something that shouldn't be within a thousand parsects of Antar; its inference would be obvious even to an investigator interested only in tax revenues. Kemmer swore at the native. The entire operation would have to be aborted now and his dreams of promotion would vanish.

"It wasn't my supply," Shifaz protested. "I was carrying it down to Karas at the mating market. He demands a pack every time he puts a show on for your silly Earthie tourists."

"You should have concealed it better."

"How was I to know that chubby slob was coming back alive? And who'd have figured that he could handle me?"

"I've told you time and again that Earthmen are tough customers when they get mad, but you had to learn it the hard way. Now we're all in the soup. The Patrol doesn't like illicit tobacco planters. Tobacco is responsible for their pay."

"But he's still in your hands and he couldn't have had time to transmit his information," Shifaz said. "You can still kill him."

Kemmer's face cleared. Sure, that was it. Delay informing the Patrol and knock the snoop off. The operation and Kemmer's future were still safe. But it irked him that he had panicked instead of thinking. It just went to show how being involved in major crime ruined the judgment. He'd have Johnson fixed up with a nice hearty meal—and he'd see that it was delivered personally. At this late date, he couldn't afford the risk of trusting a subordinate.

Kemmer's glower became a smile. The snoop's dossier indicated that he liked to eat. He should die happy.

*   *   *   *   *

With a faint click, a loaded tray passed through a slot in the rear wall of Albert Johnson's cell.

The sight and smell of Earthly cooking reminded him that he hadn't anything to eat for hours. His mouth watered as he lifted the tray and carried it to the cot. At least IC wasn't going to let him starve to death, and if this was any indication of the way they treated prisoners, an IC jail was the best place to be on this whole planet.

Since it takes a little time for substances to diffuse across the intestinal epithelium and enter the circulation, the Zark had some warning of what was about to happen from the behavior of the epithelial cells lining Albert's gut. As a result, a considerable amount of the alkaloid was stopped before it entered Albert's body—but some did pass through, for the Zark was not omnipotent.

For nearly five minutes after finishing the meal, Albert felt normally full and comfortable. Then hell broke loose. Most of the food came back with explosive violence and cramps bent him double. The Zark turned to the neutralization and elimination of the poison. Absorptive surfaces were sealed off, body fluids poured into the intestinal tract, and anti-substances formed out of Albert's energy reserve to neutralize whatever alkaloid remained.

None of the Zark's protective measures were normal to Albert's body, and with the abrupt depletion of blood glucose to supply the energy the Zark required, Albert passed into hypoglycemic shock. The Zark regretted that, but it had no time to utilize his other less readily available energy sources. In fact, there was no time for anything except the most elemental protective measures. Consequently the convulsions, tachycardia, and coma had to be ignored.

Albert's spasms were mercifully short, but when the Zark was finished, he lay unconscious on the floor, his body twitching with incoordinate spasms, while a frightened guard called in an alarm to the medics.

The Zark quivered with its own particular brand of nausea. It had not been hurt by the alkaloid, but the pain of its host left it sick with self-loathing. That it had established itself in a life-form that casually ingested deadly poisons was no excuse. It should have been more alert, more sensitive to the host's deficiencies. It had saved his life, which was some compensation, and there was much that could be done in the way of restorative and corrective measures that would prevent such a thing from occurring again—but the Zark was unhappy as it set about helping Albert's liver metabolize fat to glucose and restore blood sugar levels.

*   *   *   *   *

The medic was puzzled. She had seen some peculiar conditions at this station, but hypoglycemic shock was something new. And, being unsure of herself, she ordered Albert into the infirmary for observation. The guard, of course, didn't object, and Kemmer, when he heard of it, could only grind his teeth in frustration. He was on delicate enough ground without making it worse by not taking adequate precautions to preserve the health of his unwilling guest. Somehow that infernal snoop had escaped again....

Albert moved his head with infinite labor and looked at the intravenous apparatus dripping a colorless solution into the vein in the elbow joint of his extended left arm. He felt no pain, but his physical weakness was appalling. He could move only with the greatest effort, and the slightest exertion left him dizzy and breathless. It was obvious that he had been poisoned, and that it was a miracle of providence that he had survived. It was equally obvious that a reappraisal of his position was in order. Someone far higher up the ladder than Shifaz was responsible for this latest attempt on his life. The native couldn't possibly have reached him in the safety of IC's jail.

The implications were unpleasant. Someone important feared him enough to want him dead, which meant that his knowledge of illicit tobacco was not as secret as he thought. It would be suicide to stay in the hands of the IC any longer. Somehow he had to get out and inform the Patrol.

He looked at the intravenous drip despondently. If the solution was poisoned, there was no help for him. It was already half gone. But he didn't feel too bad, outside of being weak. It probably was all right. In any event, he would have to take it. The condition of his body wouldn't permit anything else.

He sighed and relaxed on the bed, aware of the drowsiness that was creeping over him. When he awoke, he would do something about this situation, but he was sleepy now.

*   *   *   *   *

Albert awoke strong and refreshed. He was as hungry as he always was before breakfast. Whatever was in that solution, it had certainly worked miracles. As far as he could judge, he was completely normal.

The medic was surprised to find him sitting up when she made her morning rounds. It was amazing, but this case was amazing in more ways than one. Last night he had been in a state of complete collapse, and now he was well on the road to recovery.

Albert looked at her curiously. "What was in that stuff you gave me?"

"Just dextrose and saline," she said. "I couldn't find anything wrong with you except hypoglycemia and dehydration, so I treated that." She paused and eyed him with a curiosity equal to his own. "Just what do you think happened?" she asked.

"I think I was poisoned."

"That's impossible."

"Possibly," Albert conceded, "but it might be an idea to check that food I left all over the cell."

"That was cleaned up hours ago."

"Convenient, isn't it?"

"I don't know what you mean by that," she said. "Someone in the kitchens might have made a mistake. Yet you were the only case." She looked thoughtful. "I think I will do a little checking in the Central Kitchen, just to be on the safe side." She smiled a bright professional smile. "Anyway, I'm glad to see that you have recovered so well. I'm sure you can go back tomorrow."

She vanished through the door with a rustle of white dacron. Albert, after listening a moment to make sure that she was gone, rose to his feet and began an inspection of his room.

It wasn't a jail cell. Not quite. But it wasn't designed for easy escape, either. It was on the top floor of the IC building, a good hundred feet down to the street below. The window was covered with a steel grating and the door was locked. But both window and door were designed to hold a sick man rather than a healthy and desperate one.

Albert looked out of the window. The building was constructed to harmonize with native structures surrounding it, so the outer walls were studded with protuberances and bosses that would give adequate handholds to a man strong enough to brave the terrors of the descent.

Looking down the wall, Albert wavered. Thinking back, he made up his mind.

*   *   *   *   *

Fred Kemmer was disturbed. By all the rules, Albert Johnson should be dead. But Shifaz had failed, and that fool guard *had* to call in the medics. It was going to be harder to get at Johnson, now that he was in the infirmary, but he had to be reached.

One might buy off an agent who was merely checking on tax evasion, but tobacco was another matter entirely. Kemmer wished he hadn't agreed to boss Operation Weed. The glowing dreams of promotion and fortune were beginning to yellow around the edges. Visions of the Penal Colony bothered him, for if the operation went sour, he would do the paying. He had known that when he took the job, but the possibility seemed remote then.

He shook his head. It wasn't that bad yet. As long as Johnson hadn't communicated with anyone else and as long as he was still in company hands, something could be done.

Kemmer thought a while, trying to put himself in Johnson's place. Undoubtedly the spy was frightened, and undoubtedly he would try to escape. And since it would be far easier to escape from the infirmary than it would be from detention, he would try as soon as possible.

Kemmer's face cleared. If Johnson tried it, he would find it wasn't as easy as he thought.

With characteristic swiftness, Kemmer outlined his plans and made the necessary arrangements. A guard was posted in the hall with orders to shoot if Johnson tried the door of his room, and Kemmer himself took a stand in the building across the street, facing the hospital, where he could watch the window of Albert's room. As he figured it, the window was the best bet. He stroked the long-barreled blaster lying beside him. Johnson still hadn't a chance, but these delays in disposing of him were becoming an annoyance.

Cautiously, Albert tried the grating that covered the window. The Antarian climate had rusted the heavy screws that fastened it to the casing. One of the bars was loose. If it could be removed, it would serve as a lever to pry out the entire grating.

Albert twisted at the bar. It groaned and squealed. He nervously applied more pressure, and the bar moved slowly out of its fastenings.

*   *   *   *   *

The Zark observed his actions curiously. Now why was its host twisting that rod of metal out of the woodwork? It didn't know, and it was consumed with curiosity. It had found no way to communicate with its host so that some of the man's queer actions could be understood; in the portions of the brain it had explored, there were no portals of communication. However, there still was a large dormant portion, and perhaps here lay the thing it sought. The Zark inserted a number of tendrils into the blank areas, probing, connecting synapses, opening unused pathways, looking for what it hoped existed.

The results of this action were completely unforeseen by the Zark, for it was essentially just a subordinate ego with all the lacks which that implied—and it had never before inhabited a body that possessed a potentially first-class brain. With no prior experience to draw upon, the Zark couldn't possibly guess that its actions would result in a peculiar relationship between the man and the world around him. And if the Zark had known, it probably wouldn't have cared.

Albert removed the bar and pried out the grating. With only a momentary hesitation, he lowered himself over the sill until his feet struck an ornamental knob on the wall. He glanced quickly down. There was another protuberance about two feet below the one on which he was standing. Pressing against the wall, he inched one foot downward until it found the foothold. With relief, he shifted his weight to the lower foot, and as he did a wave of heat enveloped his legs. The protuberance came loose from the wall with a grating noise mixed with the crackling hiss of a blaster bolt, and Albert plunged toward the street below.

As the pavement rushed at him, he had time for a brief, fervent wish that he were someplace else. Then the thought was swallowed in an icy blackness.

*　　*　　*　　*

Fred Kemmer lowered the blaster with a grin of satisfaction. He had figured his man correctly, and now the spy would be nothing to worry about. He watched the plummeting body—and gasped with consternation, for less than ten feet above the pavement, Albert abruptly vanished!

There is such a thing as too much surprise, too much shock, too much amazement. And that precisely was what affected Albert when he found himself standing on the street where the IC guards had picked him up. By rights, he should have been a pulpy smear against the pavement beneath the infirmary window. But he was not. He didn't question why he was here, or consider how he had managed to avoid the certain death that waited for him. The fact was that he had done it, somehow. And that was enough.

It was almost like history repeating itself. Shifaz was at his usual stand haranguing another group of tourists. It was the same spiel as before, and almost at the same point of the pitch. But his actions upon seeing Albert were entirely different. His eyes widened, but this time he slid quietly from his perch on the cornerstone of the building and disappeared into the milling crowd.

Albert followed. The fact that Shifaz was somewhere in that crowd was enough to start him moving, and, once started, stubbornness kept him going, plowing irresistibly through the thick swarm of Vaornese. Reason told him that no Earthman could expect to find a native hidden among hundreds of his own kind. Their bipedal dinosaurlike figures seemed to be cast out of one mold.

A chase through this crowd was futile, but he went on deeper into the Kazlak, drawn along an invisible trail by some unearthly sense that told him he was right. He was as certain of it as that his name was Albert Johnson. And when he finally cornered Shifaz in a deserted alley, he was the one who was not surprised.

Shifaz squawked and darted toward Albert, a knife glittering in his hand. Albert felt a stinging pain across the muscles of his left arm as he blocked the thrust aimed at his belly, wrenched the knife from the native's grasp, and slammed him to the pavement.

Shifaz bounced like a rubber ball, but he had no chance against the bigger and stronger Earthman. Albert knocked him down again. This time the native didn't rise. He lay in the street, a trickle of blood oozing from the corner of his lipless mouth, hate radiating from him in palpable waves.

Albert stood over him, panting a little from the brief but violent scuffle. "Now, Shifaz, you're going to tell me things," he said heavily.

"You can go to your Place of Punishment," Shifaz snarled. "I shall say nothing."

"I can beat the answers out of you," Albert mused aloud, "but I won't. I'll just ask you questions, and every time I don't like your answer, I'll kick one of your teeth out. If you don't answer, I guarantee that you'll look like an old grandmother."

*   *   *   *   *

Shifaz turned a paler green. To lose one's teeth was a punishment reserved only for females. He would be a thing of mockery and laughter—but there were worse things than losing teeth or face. There was such a thing as losing one's life, and he knew what would happen if he betrayed IC. Then he brightened. He could always lie, and this hulking brute of an Earthman wouldn't know—couldn't possibly know. So he nodded with a touch of artistic reluctance. "All right," he said, "I'll talk." He injected a note of fear into his voice. It wasn't hard to do.

"Where did you get that tobacco?" Albert asked.

"From a farm," Shifaz said. That was the truth. The Earthman probably knew about tobacco and there was no need to lie, yet.

"Where is it?"

Shifaz thought quickly of the clearing in the forest south of Lagash where the green broad-leaved plants were grown, and said, "It's just outside of Timargh, along the road which runs south." He waited tensely for Albert's reaction, wincing as the Earthman drew his foot back. Timargh was a good fifty miles from Lagash, and if this lie went over, he felt that he could proceed with confidence.

It went over. Albert replaced his foot on the ground. "You telling the truth?"

"As Murgh is my witness," Shifaz said with sincerity.

Albert nodded and Shifaz relaxed with hidden relief. Apparently the man knew that Murgh was the most sacred and respected deity in the pantheon of Antar, and that oaths based upon his name were inviolable. But what the scaleless oaf didn't know was that this applied to Antarians only. As far as these strangers from another world were concerned, anything went.

So Albert continued questioning, and Shifaz answered, sometimes readily, sometimes reluctantly, telling the truth when it wasn't harmful, lying when necessary. The native's brain was fertile and the tissue of lies and truth hung together well, and Albert seemed satisfied. At any rate, he finally went away, leaving behind a softly whistling Vaornese who congratulated himself on the fact that he had once more imposed upon this outlander's credulity. He was so easy to fool that it was almost a crime to do it.

But he wouldn't have been so pleased with himself if he could have seen the inside of Albert's mind. For Albert knew the truth about the four-hundred-acre farm south of Lagash. He knew about the hidden curing sheds and processing plant. He knew that both Vaornese and Lagashites were deeply involved in something they called Operation Weed, and approved of it thoroughly either from sheer cussedness or addiction. He had quietly read the native's mind while the half-truths and lies had fallen from his forked tongue. And, catching Shifaz's last thought, Albert couldn't help chuckling.

At one of the larger intersections, Albert stopped under a flaming cresset and looked at his arm. There was a wide red stain that looked black against the whiteness of his pajamas. That much blood meant more than a scratch, even though there was no pain—and cuts on this world could be deadly if they weren't attended to promptly.

He suddenly felt alone and helpless, wishing desperately for a quiet place where he could dress his wound and be safe from the eyes he knew were inspecting him. He was too conspicuous. The pajamas were out of place on the street. Undoubtedly natives were hurrying to report him to the IC.

His mind turned to his room in the hostel with its well-fitted wardrobe and its first-aid kit—and again came that instant of utter darkness—and then he was standing in the middle of his room facing the wardrobe that held his clothing.

*   *   *   *   *

He felt no surprise this time. He knew what had happened. Something within his body was acting like a tiny Distorter, transporting him through hyperspace in the same manner that a starship's engine room warped it through the folds of the normal space-time continuum. There was nothing really strange about it. It was a power which he *should* have—which any normal man should have. The fact that he didn't have it before was of no consequence, and the fact that other men didn't have it now merely made *them* abnormal.

He smiled as he considered the possibilities which these new powers gave him. They were enormous. At the very least, they tripled his value as an agent. Nothing was safe from his investigation. The most secret hiding places were open to his probings. Nothing could stop him, for command of hyperspace made a mockery of material barriers.

He chuckled happily as he removed his pajama jacket and reached for the first-aid kit. From the gash in his sleeve, there should be a nasty cut underneath, and it startled him a little that there was no greater amount of hemorrhage. He cleaned off the dried blood—and found nothing underneath except a thin red bloodless line that ran halfway around his arm. It wasn't even a scratch.

Yet he had felt Shifaz' blade slice into his flesh. He knew there was more damage than this. The blood and the slashed sleeve could tell him that, even if he didn't have the messages of his nerves. Yet now there was no pain, and the closed scratch certainly wasn't the major wound he had expected. And this *was* queer, a fact for which he had no explanation. Albert frowned. Maybe this was another facet of the psi factors that had suddenly become his.

He wondered where they had come from. Without warning, he had become able to read minds with accuracy and do an effective job of teleportation. About the only things he lacked to be a well-rounded psi were telekinetic powers and precognition.

His frown froze on his face as he became conscious of a sense of unease. They were coming down the hall—two IC guardsmen. He caught the doubt and certainty in their minds—doubt that he would be in his room, certainty that he would be ultimately caught, for on Antar there was no place for an Earthman to hide.

Albert slipped into the first suit that came to hand, blessing the seam tabs that made dressing a moment's work. As the guards opened the door, he visualized the spot on the Lagash road where he had encountered the Bandersnatch. It was easier than before. He was standing in the middle of the road, the center of the surprised attention of a few travelers, when the guards entered his room.

*   *   *   *   *

The bright light of Antar's golden day came down from a cloudless yellow sky. In the forest strip ahead, Albert could hear a faint medley of coughs, grunts and snarls as the lesser beasts fed upon the remains of yesterday's garbage. Albert moved down the road, ignoring the startled natives. This time he wasn't afraid of meeting a Bandersnatch or anything else, for he had a method of escape that was foolproof. Lagash was some thirty miles ahead, but in the lighter gravity of Antar, the walk would be stimulating rather than exhausting.

He went at a steady pace, occasionally turning his glance to the road, impressing sections of it upon his memory so that he could return to them via teleport if necessary. He found that he could memorize with perfect ease. Even the positions of clumps of grass and twigs were remembered with perfect clarity and in minute detail. The perfection of his memory astonished and delighted him.

The Zark felt pleased with itself. Although it had never dreamed of the potential contained in the host's mind, it realized that it was responsible for the release of these weird powers, and it enjoyed the new sensations and was eager for more. If partial probing could achieve so much, what was the ultimate power of this remarkable mind? The Zark didn't know, but, like a true experimenter, it was determined to find out—so it probed deeper, opening still more pathways and connecting more synapses with the conscious brain.

It was routine work that could be performed automatically while the rest of the Zark enjoyed the colorful beauty of the Antarian scenery.

With the forest quickly left behind him, Albert walked through gently rolling grassland dotted with small farms and homesteads. It was a peaceful scene, similar to many he had seen on Earth, and the familiarity brought a sense of nostalgic longing to be home again. But the feeling was not too strong, more intellectual than physical, for the memories of Earth were oddly blurred.

Time passed and the road unreeled behind him. Once he took to the underbrush to let a humming IC ground car pass, and twice more he hid as airboats swept by overhead, but the annoyances were minor and unimportant.

When hiding from the second airboat, he disturbed a kelit in the thick brush growing beside the road. The little insect-eater chittered in alarm and dashed off to safety across the highway. And Albert, looking at it, was conscious not only of the external shape but the internal as well!

He could see its little heart pounding in its chest, and the pumping bellows of the pink lungs that surrounded it. He was aware of the muscles pulling and relaxing as the kelit ran, and the long bones sliding in their lubricated joints. He saw the tenseness of the abdominal organs, felt the blind fear in the creature's mind. The totality of his impressions washed through him with a clear wave of icy shock.

*   *   *   *   *

Grimly, he shrugged it off. He had ESP. He ought to have expected it—it was the next logical step. He scrambled back to the road and walked onward a little faster, until the battlements of Lagash came in sight.

The Lagash Arm was farther from the city than was that of Vaornia, and as he came to the strip of jungle, he turned his eyes upon the empty parklike arcades between the trees. The last edible garbage had long since been consumed and the greater and lesser beasts had departed for the cooler depths of the forest, but Albert was conscious of life. It was all around him, in the trees with the ringed layers of their trunks and the sap flowing slowly upward through the cambium layer beneath their scaly bark, in the insects feeding upon the nectar of the aerial vine blossoms, in the rapid photosynthetic reactions of the leaves.

His gaze, turning aloft, was conscious of the birds and the tiny arboreal mammals. He saw the whole forest with eyes filled with wonder at its life and beauty. It was the only right way to see.

At the proper distance from Lagash, he plunged off boldly across country and entered the main area of the forest, reflecting wryly as he did so that he was probably the first human in the short history of Antarian exploration who had gone into one of the great forests with absolute knowledge that he would come out of it alive. And, as so often happens to men who have no fear, trouble avoided him.

He followed the directions he had obtained from Shifaz and found the plantation without trouble. He could hardly miss it, because its size was far from accurately expressed in the native's memory. Skillfully concealed beneath an overhanging network of aerial vines whose camouflage made it invisible from the air, concealing the tobacco plants from casual detector search, the plantation extended in row upon narrow row, the irregular strips of fields separated by rows of trees from which the camouflage was hung. A fragile electric fence encircled the area, a seemingly weak defense, but one through which even the greatest Antarian beast would not attempt to pass.

Albert whistled softly under his breath at what he saw, recorded it in his memory. Then, having finished the eyewitness part of his task, he recalled a section of road over which he had passed, and pushed.

The return journey to Vaornia was experimental in nature, as Albert tried the range of his powers. His best was just short of twenty miles and the journey which had taken him eight hours was made back in somewhat less than twenty minutes, counting half a dozen delays and backtracks.

*   *   *   *   *

There was no question about where Albert would go next. He had to get evidence, and that evidence lay in only one place—in the local office of the Interworld Corporation in Vaornia.

A moment later, he stood in the reception room looking across the empty desks at the bright square of light shining through the glassite paneled door of Fred Kemmer's office. It was past closing hours, but Kemmer had a right to be working late. Right now, he was probably sweating blood at the thought of what would happen if Albert had finally managed to escape him. The Corporation would virtuously disown him and leave him to face a ten-year rap in Penal Colony. Albert almost felt sorry for him.

Albert let his perception sense travel through the wall and into Kemmer's room. His guess was right—the local boss was sweating.

He checked Kemmer's office swiftly, but the only thing that interested him was the big vault beside the desk. He visualized the interior of the vault and pushed himself inside. Separated from Kemmer by six inches of the hardest metal known to Man, he quietly leafed through the files of confidential correspondence until he found what he wanted. He didn't need a light. His perception worked as well in the dark as in the daylight.

There was enough documentary evidence in the big vault to indict quite a few more IC officials than Kemmer—and perhaps investigation of *their* files would provide more leads to even higher officials. Wherever Kemmer was going, Albert had the idea that he wouldn't be going alone.

Albert selected all the incriminating letters and documents he could find and packed the micro-files in his jacket. Finally, bulging with documentary information, he pushed back into the streets.

It was late enough for few natives to be on the streets, and his appearance caused no comment. Apparently unnoticed, he moved rapidly into the Kazlak, searching for a place to hide the papers he had stolen. What he had learned of Vaornia made him cautious. He checked constantly for spies, but there wasn't a native in sensing range.

He ducked into the alleyway where he had caught Shifaz. His memory of it had been right. There was a small hole in one of the building walls, partly covered with cracked plaster, and barely visible in the darkness. The gloom of the Kazlak scarcely varied with night or day, as the enormous labyrinth of covered passages and building walls was pierced with only a few ventilation holes. Cressets at the main intersections burned constantly, their smokeless flames lighting the streets poorly.

He wondered idly how he had managed to remember the way to this place, let alone the little hole in the wall, as he stuffed the micro-files into its dark interior. He finished, turned to leave, and was out on the main tunnel before he became aware of the IC ground cars closing in upon him.

The Corporation was really on the beam, their spies everywhere. But they didn't know his abilities. He visualized and pushed. They were going to be surprised when he vanished—but he didn't vanish.

The expression of shocked surprise was still on his face as the stat gun blast took him squarely in the chest.

* * * * *

He was tied to a chair in Fred Kemmer's office. He recognized it easily, although physically he had never been inside the room. His head hurt as a polygraph recorder was strapped to his left arm, and behind him, beyond his range of vision, he could sense another man and several machines. In front of him stood Fred Kemmer with an expression of satisfaction on his face.

"Don't start thinking you're smart," Kemmer said. "You're in no position for it."

"You've tried to kill me three times," Albert reminded him.

"There's always a fourth time."

"I don't think so. Too many people know."

"Precisely my own conclusion," Kemmer said, "but there are other ways. Brainwashing's a good one."

"That's illegal!" Albert protested. "Besides—"

"So what?" Kemmer cut him off. "It's an illegal universe."

Albert probed urgently at the IC man's mind, hoping to find something he could turn to his advantage, but all he found were surface thoughts—satisfaction at having gotten the spy where he could do no harm, plans for turning Albert into a mindless idiot, thoughts of extracting information—all of which had an air of certainty that was unnerving. Albert had badly underestimated him. It was high time to leave here, if he could.

Albert visualized an area outside Vaornia, and, as he tried to push, a machine hummed loudly behind him. He didn't move. Mistake, Albert thought worriedly, I'm not going anywhere—and he knows I'm scared.

"It won't do you any good," Kemmer said. "It didn't take too much brains to figure you were using hyperspace in those disappearing acts. There's an insulating field around that chair that'd stop a space yacht." He leaned forward. "Now—what are your contacts, and who gave you the information on where to look?"

Albert saw no reason to hide it, but there was no sense in revealing anything. The Patrol had word of his arrest by now and should be here any moment.

It was as though Kemmer had read his mind. "Don't count on being rescued. I stopped the Patrol report." Kemmer paused, obviously enjoying the expression on Albert's face. "You know," he went on, "there's a peculiar fact about nerves that maybe you don't know. A stimulus sets up a brief neural volley lasting about a hundredth of a second. Following that comes a period of refractivity lasting perhaps a tenth of that time while the nerve repolarizes, and then, immediately after repolarization, there is an extremely short period of hypersensitivity."

"What's that to do with me?" Albert asked.

"You'll find out if you don't answer promptly and truthfully. That gadget on your arm is connected to a polygraph. Now do you want to make a statement?"

Albert shook his head. He was conscious of a brief pain in one finger, and the next instant someone tore the finger out of his hand with red hot pincers. He screamed. He couldn't help it. This punishment was beyond agony.

"Nice, isn't it?" Kemmer asked as Albert looked down at his amputated finger that still was remarkably attached to his hand. "And the beauty of it is that it doesn't even leave a mark. Of course, if it's repeated enough, it will end up as a permanent paralysis of the part stimulated. Now once again—who gave you that information?"

*   *   *   *   *

Albert talked. It was futile to try to deceive a polygraph and he wanted no more of that nerve treatment—and then he looked into Kemmer's mind again and discovered what went into brainwashing. The shock was like ice water. Hypersensitive stimulation, Kemmer was thinking gleefully, would reduce this fat slob in the chair to a screaming mindless lump that could be molded like wet putty.

Albert felt helpless. He couldn't run and he couldn't fight. But he wasn't ready to give up. His perception passed over and through Kemmer with microscopic care, looking for some weakness, something that could be exploited to advantage. Kemmer *had* to have a vulnerable point.

He did.

There was a spot on the inner lining of the radial vein in Kemmer's left arm. He had recently received an inoculation, one of the constant immunizing injections that were necessary on Antar, for there was a small thrombus clinging to the needle puncture on the inner wall of the vessel. Normally it was unimportant and would pass away in time and be absorbed, but there were considerable possibilities for trouble in that little blob of red cells and fibrin if they could be loosened from their attachment to the wall.

Hopefully, Albert reached out. If he couldn't move himself, perhaps he could move the clot.

The thrombus stirred and came free, rushing toward Kemmer's heart. Albert followed it, watching as it passed into the pulmonary artery, tracing it out through the smaller vessels until it stopped squarely across a junction of two arterioles.

Kemmer coughed, his face whitening with pain as he clutched at his chest. The pain was a mild repayment for his recent agony, Albert thought grimly. A pulmonary embolism shouldn't kill him, but the effects were disproportionate to the cause and would last a while. He grinned mercilessly as Kemmer collapsed.

A man darted from behind the chair and bent over Kemmer. Fumbling in his haste, he produced a pocket communicator, stabbed frantically at the dial and spoke urgently into it. "Medic! Boss's office—hurry!"

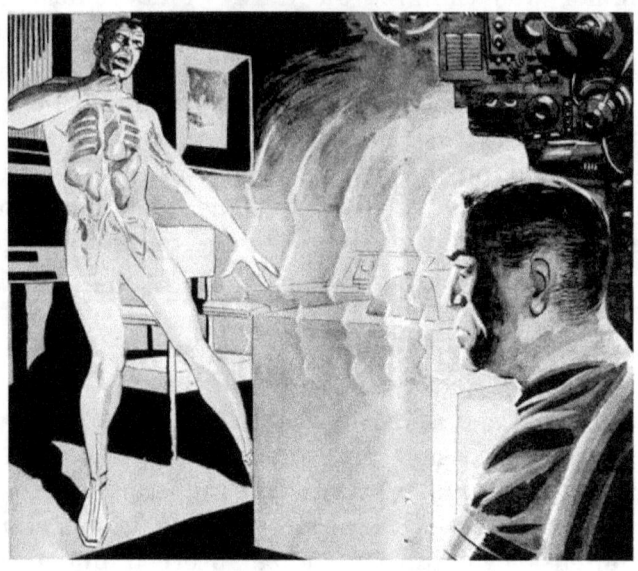

For a second, Albert didn't realize that the hum of machinery behind him had stopped, but when he did, both Albert and the chair vanished.

The Zark realized that its host had been hurt again. It was infuriating to be so helpless. Things kept happening to Albert which it couldn't correct until too late. There were forces involved that it didn't know how to handle; they were entirely outside the Zark's experience. It only felt relief when Albert managed to regain his ability to move—and, as it looked out upon the familiar green Antarian countryside, it felt almost happy. Of course Albert was probably still in trouble, but it wasn't so bad now. At least the man was away from the cause of his pain.

*   *   *   *   *

It was a hell of a note, Albert reflected, sitting beside the road that led to Lagash and working upon the bonds that tied him to the chair. He had managed to get out of Kemmer's hands, but it appeared probable that he would get no farther. As things stood, he couldn't transmit the information he had gained—and by this time probably every IC office on the planet was alerted to the fact that Earth Central had a psi-type agent on Antar—one who was not inherently unstable, like those poor devils in the parapsychological laboratories on Earth. They would be ready for him with everything from Distorter screens to Kellys.

He didn't underestimate IC now. Whatever its morals might be, its personnel was neither stupid nor slow to act. He was trapped in this sector of the planet. Prime Base was over a thousand miles away, and even if he did manage to make his way back to it along the trade routes, it was a virtual certainty that he would never be able to get near a class I communicator or the Patrol office. IC would have ample time to get ready for him, and no matter what powers he possessed, a single man would have no chance against the massed technology of the corporation.

However, he could play tag with IC in this area for some time with the reasonable possibility that he wouldn't get caught. If nothing else, it would have nuisance value. He pulled one hand free of the tape that held it to the chair arm and swiftly removed the rest of the tape that bound him. He had his freedom again. Now what would he do with it?

He left the chair behind and started down the road toward Lagash. There was no good reason to head in that particular direction, but at the moment one direction was as good as another until he could plan a course of action. His brain felt oddly fuzzy. He didn't realize that he had reached the end of his strength until he dropped in the roadway.

To compensate for the miserable job it had done in protecting him from poison and neural torture, the Zark had successfully managed to block hunger and fatigue pains until Albert's over-taxed body could stand no more. It realized its error after Albert collapsed. Sensibly, it did nothing. Its host had burned a tremendous amount of energy without replenishment, and he needed time to rest and draw upon less available reserves, and to detoxify and eliminate the metabolic poisons in his body.

It was late that afternoon before Albert recovered enough to take more than a passing interest in his surroundings. He had a vague memory of hiring a dak cart driver to take him down the road. The memory was apparently correct, because he was lying in the back of a cargo cart piled high with short pieces of cane. The cart was moving at a brisk pace despite the apparently leisurely movements of the dak between the shafts. The ponderous ten-foot strides ate up distance.

He was conscious of a hunger that was beyond discomfort, and a thirst that left his mouth dry and cottony. It was as though he hadn't eaten or drunk for days. He felt utterly spent, drained beyond exhaustion. He was in no shape to do anything, and unless he managed to find food and drink pretty soon, he would be easy pickings for IC.

*   *   *   *   *

He looked around the cart, but there was nothing except the canes on which he lay. There wasn't even any of the foul porridgelike mess that the natives called food, since native workers didn't bother about eating during working hours.

He turned over slowly, feeling the hard canes grind into his body as he moved. He kept thinking about food— about meals aboard ship, about dinners, about Earth restaurants, about steak, potatoes, bread—solid heartening foods filled with proteins, fats and carbohydrates.

Carbohydrates—the thought stuck in his mind for some reason. And then he realized why.

The canes he was lying on in in the cart were sugar cane! He had never seen them on Earth, but he should have expected to find them out here—one of Earth's greatest exports was the seeds from which beet and cane sugar were obtained.

He pulled a length of cane from the pile and bit into one end. His depleted body reached eagerly for the sweet energy that filled his mouth.

With the restoration of his energy balance came clearer and more logical thought. It might be well enough to make IC spend valuable time looking for him, but such delaying actions had no positive value. Ultimately he would be caught, and his usefulness would disappear with his death. But if he could get word to the Patrol, this whole business could be smashed.

Now if he made a big enough disturbance—it might possibly even reach the noses of the Patrol. Perhaps by working through the hundred or so tourists in Vaornia and Lagash, he could—

That was it, the only possible solution. The IC might be able to get rid of one man, but it couldn't possibly get rid of a hundred—and somewhere in that group of tourists there would be one who'd talk, someone who would pass the word. IC couldn't keep this quiet without brainwashing the lot of them, and that in itself would be enough to bring a Patrol ship here at maximum blast.

He chuckled happily. The native driver, startled at the strange sound, turned his head just in time to see his passenger vanish, together with a bundle of cane. The native shook his head in an oddly human gesture. These foreigners were strange creatures indeed.

*   *   *   *   *

Albert, thin, pale, but happy, sat at a table in one of the smaller cafeterias in Earth Center, talking to the Chief over a second helping of dessert. The fearful energy drain of esper activity, combined with the constant dodging to avoid IC hunting parties, had made him a gaunt shadow—but he had managed to survive until a Patrol ship arrived to investigate the strange stories told by tourists, of a man who haunted the towns of Lagash and Vaornia, and the road between.

"That's all there was to it, sir," Albert concluded. "Once I figured it out that not even IC could get away with mass murder, it was easy. I just kept popping up in odd places and telling my story, and then, to make it impressive, I'd disappear. I had nearly two days before IC caught on, and by then you knew. The only trouble was getting enough to eat. I damn near starved before the Patrol arrived. I expect that we owe quite a few farmers and shopkeepers reparations for the food I stole."

"They'll be paid, providing they present a claim," the Chief said. "But there's one thing about all this that bothers me. I know you had no psi powers when you left Earth on this mission, just where did you acquire them?"

Albert shook his head. "I don't know," he said. "Unless they were latent and developed in Antar's peculiar climatic and physical conditions. Or maybe it was the shock of that meeting with the Bandersnatch. All I'm sure of is that I didn't have any until after that meeting with Shifaz."

"Well, you certainly have them now. The Parapsych boys are hot on your tail, but we've stalled them off."

"Thanks. I don't want to imitate a guinea pig."

"We owe you at least that for getting us a case against IC. Even their shysters won't be able to wiggle out of this one." The Chief smiled. "It's nice to have those lads where they can be handled for a change."

"They do need a dose of applied conscience," Albert agreed.

"The government also owes you a bonus and a vote of thanks."

"I'll appreciate the bonus," Albert said as he signaled for the waitress. "Recently, I can't afford my appetite."

"It's understandable. After all, you've lost nearly eighty pounds."

"Wonder if I'll ever get them back," Albert muttered as he bit into the third dessert.

The Chief watched enviously. "I wouldn't worry about that," he said. "Just get your strength back. There's another assignment for you, one that will need your peculiar talents." He stood up. "I'll be seeing you. My ulcer can't take your appetite any more." He walked away.

Inside Albert, the Zark alerted. A new assignment! That meant another world and new sensations. Truly, this host was magnificent! It had been a lucky day when he had fallen in running from the Bandersnatch. The Zark quivered with delight—

And Albert felt it.

Turning his perception inward to see what might be wrong, he saw the Zark for the first time.

* * * * *

For a second, a wave of repulsion swept through his body, but as he comprehended the extent of that protoplasmic mass so inextricably intertwined with his own, he realized that this thing within him was the reason for his new powers. There could be no other explanation.

And as he searched farther, he marveled. The Zark was unspecialized in a way he had never imagined—an amorphous aggregation of highly evolved cells that could imitate normal tissues in a manner that would defy ordinary detection. It was something at once higher yet lower than his own flesh, something more primitive yet infinitely more evolved.

The Zark had succeeded at last. It had established communication with its host.

"Answer me, parasite," Albert muttered subvocally. "I know you're there—and I know you can answer!"

The Zark gave the protean equivalent of a shrug. If Albert only knew how it had tried to communicate—no, there was no communication between them. Their methods of thought were so different that there was no possible rapport.

It twitched—and Albert jumped. And for the first time in its long life, the Zark had an original idea. It moved a few milligrams of its substance to Albert's throat region, and after a premonitory glottal spasm, Albert said very distinctly and quite involuntarily, "All right. I am here."

Albert froze with surprise, but when the shock passed, he laughed. "Well, I asked for it," he said. "But it's like the story about the man who talked to himself—and got answers. Not exactly a comforting sensation."

"I'm sorry," the Zark apologized. "I do not wish to cause discomfort."

"You pick a poor way to keep from doing it."

"It was the only way I could figure to make contact with your conscious mind—and you desired that I communicate."

"I suppose you're right. But while it is nice to know that I really have a guardian angel, I'd have felt better about it if you had white robes and wings and were hovering over my shoulder."

"I don't understand," the Zark said.

"I was trying to be funny. You know," Albert continued after a moment, "I never thought of trying to perceive myself. I wonder why. I guess because none of the medical examinations showed anything different from normal."

"I was always afraid that you might suspect before I could tell you," the Zark replied. "It was an obvious line of reasoning, and you *are* an intelligent entity—the most intelligent I have ever inhabited. It is too bad that I shall have to leave. I have enjoyed being with you."

"Who said anything about leaving?" Albert asked.

"You did. I could feel your revulsion when you became aware of me. It wasn't nice, but I suppose you can't help it. Yours is an independent race, one that doesn't willingly support—" the voice hesitated as though searching for the proper word—"fellow travelers," it finished.

Albert grinned. "There are historical precedents for that statement, but your interpretation isn't quite right. I was surprised. You startled me."

He fell silent, and the Zark, respecting the activity of his mind, forbore to interrupt.

*   *   *   *   *

Albert was doing some heavy thinking about the Zark. Certainly it had protected him on Antar, and with equal certainty it must have been responsible for the psi owners he possessed. He owed it a lot, for without its help he wouldn't have survived.

There was only one thing wrong.

Sexless though it was, the Zark must possess the characteristics of life, since it was obviously alive. And those characteristics were unchanging throughout the known universe. The four vital criteria defined centuries ago were still as good today as they were then—growth, metabolism, irritability—and *reproduction*. Despite its lack of sex, the Zark must be capable of producing others of its kind, and while he didn't mind supporting one fellow traveler, he was damned if he'd support a whole family of them.

"That need never bother you," the Zark interrupted. "As an individual, I am very long-lived and seldom reproduce. I can, of course, but the process is quite involved—actually it involves making a twin out of myself—and it is not necessary. Besides, there cannot be two Zarks in one host. My offspring would have to seek another."

"And do they have your powers?"

"Of course. They would know all I know, for a Zark's memory is not concentrated in specialized tissue like your brain."

A light began to dawn in Albert's mind. Maybe this was the answer to the corporate conscience he had been wishing for so wistfully on Antar. "Does it bother you to reproduce?" he asked.

"It is annoying, but not painful—nor would it be too difficult after a pattern was set in my cells. But why do you ask this?"

"The thought just occurred to me that there are quite a few people who could use a Zark. A few of the more honest folks would improve this Confederation's moral tone if they had the power—and certainly psi powers in law enforcement would be unbeatable."

"Then you would want me to reproduce?"

"It might be a good idea if we can find men who are worthy of Zarks. I could check them with my telepathy and perhaps we might—"

"Let me warn you," the Zark interjected. "While this all sounds very fine, there are difficulties, even with a host as large as yourself. I shall need more energy than your body has available in order to duplicate myself. It will be hard for you to do what must be done."

"And what is that?"

"Eat," the Zark said, "great quantities of high energy foods." It shuddered at the thought of Albert overloading his digestive tract any more than he had been doing the past week.

But Albert's reaction went to prove that while their relationship was physically close, mentally they were still far apart. Albert, the Zark noted in astonishment, didn't regard it as an ordeal at all.

The Issahar Artifacts

Originally Published Amazing Science Fiction Stories, April 1960

Lincoln said it eons ago....
It took a speck of one-celled plant life on a world
parsecs away to prove it for all the galaxy.

The Issahar Artifacts

The following manuscript was discovered during the excavation of a lateral connecting link between the North-South streamways in Narhil Province near Issahar on Kwashior. The excavator, while passing through a small valley about 20 yursts south of the city, was jammed by a mass of oxidized and partially oxidized metallic fragments. On most worlds this would not be unusual, but Kwashior has no recorded history of metallic artifacts. The terrestrial operator, with unusual presence of mind, reported the stoppage immediately. Assasul, the District Engineering monitor, realized instantly that no metallic debris should exist in that area, and in consequence ordered a most careful excavation in the event that the artifacts might have cultural significance.

The debris proved to be the remnants of an ancient spaceship similar to those described in Sector Chronicles IV through VII, but of much smaller size and cruder design—obviously a relic of pre-expansion days. Within the remnants of the ship was found a small box of metal covered with several thicknesses of tar and wax impregnated fabric which had been mostly destroyed. The metal itself was badly oxidized, but served to protect an inner wooden box that contained a number of thin sheets of a fragile substance composed mainly of cellulose which were brown and crumbling with age. The sheets were covered with runes of *lingua antiqua* arranged in regular rows, inscribed by hand with a carbon-based ink which has persisted remarkably well despite the degenerative processes of time. Although much of the manuscript is illegible, sufficient remains to settle for all time the Dannar-Marraket Controversy and lend important corroborating evidence to the Cassaheb Thesis of Terrestrial migrations.

The genuineness of this fragment has been established beyond doubt. Radiocarbon dating places its age at ten thousand plus or minus one hundred cycles, which would place it at the very beginning of the Intellectual Emergence. Its importance is beyond question. Its implications are shocking despite the fact that they conform to many of the early legends and form a solid foundation for Dannar's Thesis which has heretofore been regarded as implausible. In the light of this material, the whole question of racial origins may well have to be reevaluated. Without further comment, the translated text is presented herewith. You may draw your own conclusions. Go with enlightenment.

-BARRAGOND-
Monitor of Cultural Origins and Relics Kwashior Central Repository

*   *   *   *   *

I have decided after some thought, to write this journal. It is, I suppose, a form of egotism—for I do not expect that it shall ever be read in the event that I am unable to leave this place. Yet it affords me a certain satisfaction to think that a part of me will remain long after I have returned to dust. In any event, I feel that one is not truly dead if a part of his personality remains. Many of the ancients such as Homer, Phidias, Confucius, Christ, da Vinci, Lincoln, Einstein, Churchill—and many others—live on through their works when otherwise they would long since have been forgotten and thus be truly dead. Earth's history is full of such examples. And while I have no expectation of an immortality such as theirs, it flatters my ego to think that there will be some part of me which also will survive ...

(Note: There are several lines following this which are obliterated, defaced or unreadable. There are more to

follow. In the future such gaps in the content will be indicated thus: ...)

... I expect that it is a basic trait of character, for spacemen must be gregarious, and although I am not truly a spaceman I have been in space and, in consequence, my character is no different from my ex-crewmates—at least in that respect. I think as time passes I shall miss the comfort of companionship, the sense of belonging to a group, the card games, the bull sessions, the endless speculation on what comes next, or what we will do when the voyage is over and we are again on Earth ...

... I particularly recall Gregory. Odd, but I never knew his surname, or maybe it was his given name, for Gregory could function as well in one respect as the other. He would boast continually of what he would do to wine, women, and song once we returned to Earth. Poor Gregory. The meteor that hulled our ship struck squarely through the engine room where he was on duty. Probably he never knew that he had died. At least his fate had the mercy of being brief. Certainly it is not like mine. It was ... given ...

There was plenty of time for the survivors to reach the lifeboats, and in our decimated condition there were plenty of boats—which increased our chances of living by a factor of four ... I suppose that it was foolish to give way to the feeling of every man for himself but I am not a spaceman trained to react automatically to emergencies. Neither am I a navigator or a pilot, although I can fly in an emergency. I am a biologist, a specialist member of the scientific staff—essentially an individualist. I knew enough to seal myself in, push the eject button and energize the drive. However, I did not know that a lifeboat had no acceleration compensators, and by the time the drive lever returned to neutral, I was far out in space and thoroughly lost. I could detect no lifeboats in the vicinity nor could I raise any on the radio. I later found that a transistor malfunctioned, but by then I was well out of range, stranded between the stars in the black emptiness of space. After reading the manual on lifeboat operation there was but one course open. I selected the nearest G-type star, set the controls on automatic, and went into cold sleep. There was nothing else to do. If I remained awake I would be dead of oxygen starvation long before I reached a habitable world. The only alternative was the half-death of frozen sleep and the long wait until the boat came within range of the sun I had selected.

*   *   *   *   *

I awoke in orbit around this world, and after I recovered full use of my faculties and checked the analyzer, I decided to land. I'm afraid I did a rather bad job of it, since I used the chemical rockets too late, and the plasma jets scorched a considerable amount of acreage in the meadow where I finally came to rest. However, the residual radioactivity is low, and it is safe enough to walk outside.... The life boat is lying beside a small stream which empties into a circular pool of blue water in the center of a small meadow. The fiery trail of the jets and rockets has burned a hundred-foot-wide path across the meadow, and the upper edge of the pool, and ends in a broad, blackened circle surrounding the boat. I came down too fast the last few feet, and the drive tubes are a crumpled mess inextricably fused with the bent landing pads. This boat will never fly again without extensive repairs which I cannot perform. But the hull is otherwise sound, and I am comfortable enough except for a few rapidly healing bruises and contusions. In a few days I should be well enough to explore....

I am surprised that this world is so capable of supporting human life. The consensus of scientific opinion has been that less than one out of 50,000 planets would be habitable. Yet I have struck paydirt on the first try. Perhaps I am lucky. At any rate I am alive, and my lifeboat, while somewhat damaged by an inept landing, is still sufficiently intact to serve as a shelter, and the survival kits are undamaged, which should make my stay here endurable if not pleasant ... and we are learning a great deal about our galaxy with the development of the interstellar drive—not the least of which is that authoritative opinion is mere opinion and far from authoritative.

This world on which I find myself is in every respect but one similar to Earth. There is no animate life—only plants. No birds fly, no insects buzz, no animals rustle the silent underbrush. The only noise is the wind in the trees and grasses. I am utterly alone. It is a strange feeling, this loneliness. There is a feeling of freedom in it, a release from the too-close proximity of my fellow men. There is the pleasure of absolute privacy. But this will undoubtedly pall. Already I find that I am anxious for someone to talk to, someone with whom I can share ideas and plans. There ...

... which I cannot explain. But one thing is certain. My first impression of this place was wrong. The life here, if not animate, is at least intelligent—and it is not friendly. Yet neither does it hate. It observes me with a slow, methodical curiosity that I can sense at the very threshold of consciousness. It is a peculiar sensation that is quite indescribable—unpleasant—but hardly terrifying. I suppose I can feel it more than a normal person because I am a biologist and it is part of my training and specialized skill to achieve a certain rapport with my surroundings. I first noticed it yesterday. It came suddenly, without warning, a vague uneasiness, like the feeling when one awakens from a partially remembered but unpleasant dream. And it has been increasing ever since.

*   *   *   *   *

The principal impressions I received from this initial contact were an awareness of self and a recognizance of identity—the concept of *cogito ergo sum* came through quite clearly. I wonder what Descartes would think of an alien intelligence quoting his dogma.... I think it is animal, despite the absence of animal life in this area. The thought patterns are quick and flexible. And they have been increasing in power and precision at an appreciable rate. I am sure that it is aware of me. I shall call the feeling "it" until I can identify the source more accurately. Certainly "it" appears to be as good a description as any, since there is no consciousness of sex in the thought patterns. I wonder what sort of ... and to my surprise I *swore*! I do not ordinarily curse or use obscenities—not because they are obscene but because they are a poor and inexact means of conveying ideas or impressions. But in this case they were particularly appropriate. No other words could so precisely describe my feelings. Me, a rational intelligence, succumbing to such low-level emotional stimuli! If this keeps on, the next thing I know I will be seeing little green men flitting through the trees.... Of course, this world is unnatural, which makes its effect on the nervous system more powerful, yet that does not explain the feeling of tension which I have been experiencing, the silent straining tension of an overloaded cable, the tension of a toy balloon overfull with air. I have a constant feeling of dreadful expectancy, of imminent disaster, mixed with a sense of pain and a lively—almost childlike—curiosity. To say that this is disquieting would be a complete understatement, this state of chronic disease, mixed with occasional rushes of terror. I am certain that my nervous system and emotional responses are being examined, and catalogued like a visceral preparation in an anatomy laboratory. There is something infinitely chilling about this mental dissection.

... and after a careful search of the area I found precisely nothing. You who may read this will probably laugh, but I cannot. To me this is no laughing matter. I find myself jumping at the slightest noise, an increase in the wind, the snap of an expanding hull plate, the crackle of static over my radio. I whirl around to see who, or *what*, is watching me. My skin crawls and prickles as though I were covered with ants. My mind is filled with black, inchoate dread. In three words, *I'm scared stiff!* Yet there is nothing tangible—nothing I should be frightened about, and this terrifies me even more. For I know where this continual fear and worry can lead—to what ends this incessant stimulation can reach.

* * * * *

Under pressure my body reacts, preparing me to fight or flee. My adrenals pump hormones into my bloodstream, stimulating my heart and my sympathetic nervous system, making glucose more available to my muscles. My peripheral capillaries dilate. Intestinal activity stops as blood is channeled into the areas which my fear and my glands decide will need it most. I sweat. My vision blurs. All the manifold changes of the fight or flight syndrome are mobilized for instant action. But my body cannot be held in this state of readiness. The constant stimulation will ultimately turn my overworked adrenal glands into a jelly-like mess of cystic quivering goo. My general adaptation syndrome will no longer adapt. And I will die.

But I am not dead yet. And I have certain advantages. I am intelligent. I know what faces me. And I can adjust. That is one of the outstanding characteristics of the human race—the ability to adjust to our environment, or, failing that, to adjust our environment to us. In addition, I have my hands, tools, and materials to work with here in the lifeboat. And finally I am desperate! I should be able to accomplish something. There must be ...

* * * * *

... But it is not going well. There are too many parts which I do not know by sight. If I were a more competent electronicist I would have had the parts assembled now and would be sending a beacon signal clear across this sector. The pressure hasn't been any help. It doesn't get greater, but it has become more insisting—more demanding. I seem to feel that it *wants* something, that its direction has become more channelized. The conviction is growing within me that I am destined to be *absorbed*.

The fear with which I live is a constant thing. And I still keep looking for my enemy. In a strange, impersonal way it has become my enemy for though it does not hate, it threatens my life. My waking hours are hell and my sleep is nightmare. Strange how a man clings to life and sanity. It would be so easy to lose either. Of one thing I am certain—this cannot go on much longer. I cannot work under pressure. I must act. I shall try again to find my enemy and kill it before it kills me. It is no longer a question of ...

... Never again shall I wish to be alone. If I get out of this alive I am going to haunt crowds. I will surround myself with people. Right now I would give my soul to have one—just one—person near me. Anyone. I feel certain that two of us could face this thing and lick it. If necessary we could face it back to back, each covering the other. I am now getting impressions. Sensory hallucinations. I am floating. I swim. I bathe luxuriantly in huge bathtubs and the water runs through my body as though I were a sponge. Have you ever felt *porous*?...

... and that last attack was a doozer! I wrecked a week's work looking for the little man who wasn't there. The urge to kill is becoming more intense. I want to destroy the author of my misery. Even though I am still a balanced personality—polite language for being sane—I can't take much more of this. I will not go mad, but I will go into the adrenal syndrome unless I can end this soon.

Nothing I have done seems to help. For a while I was sure that the music tapes held the pressure back, but the enemy is used to them now. I am still working on the subspace beacon. The radio and most of the control linkages have gone into it. It looks like an electronicist's nightmare, but if the survival manual is right, it will work. It has to work! I dread the time when I shall have to cannibalize the recorder. Can't help thinking that Shakespeare was right when he wrote that bit about music soothing the savage breast. It may not soothe the enemy, for it isn't savage, but it certainly soothes me, even though there's something repetitive about it after a half a hundred playings. My breast's savage all right. Fact is, it's downright primitive when an attack starts. I can feel them coming now. I keep wondering how much longer I can last. Guess I'm getting morbid....

More nightmares last night. I drowned three times and a purple octopus gave me an enema. Woke up screaming, but got an idea from it. Funny that I never thought of it before. Water's the fountainhead of life, and there is no real reason for assuming my enemy is terrestrial. He could just as well be aquatic. I'll find out today—maybe. Just to be doing something positive—even thinking—makes me feel better....

*   *   *   *   *

Got it! I know where it is! And I know how to kill it. Fact is, I've already done it! Now there's no more pressure. God—what a relief! This morning I burned the meadow and cut down the nearest trees surrounding this clearing and nothing happened. I expected that. Then I checked the water. Nothing in the stream, but the pond was *green!*—filled almost to the edge with a mass of algae! A hundred-foot platter of sticky green slime, cohesive as glue and ugly as sin. It *had* to be it—and it was. I never saw algae that cohered quite like that. So I gave it about fifty gallons of rocket juice—red fuming nitric acid—right in the belly. Then I sat down and let the tension flow out of me, revelling in its pain, laughing like crazy as it turned brown—and the pressure disappeared. No tension at all now. The place is as quiet and peaceful as the grave. I want to laugh and laugh—and run through the burned meadow and roll in the ashes so grateful am I for my deliverance.

Got the idea of killing the monster from a splash of rocket fuel on the bank of the stream and my memory of the pain in the early feelings. But it was nothing compared to the feeling when the acid hit that damned mass of green slime! Even though my brain was screaming at me, I felt good. I should put a couple of hundred gallons into the stream just to make sure—but I can't afford it. I need the fuel to run the generators to propagate the wave that'll bring me home if someone hears it. And they'll hear it all right. My luck is in. Now I'm going to sleep—*sweet sleep that knits the ravelled sleeve of care*—Shakespeare, old man, you had a phrase for everything! I love you. I love everything. I even feel sorry for that poor plant ... of guilt. It couldn't help the fact that my jets set up a mutation. And being intelligent it *had* to be curious. Of course, no one would believe me if I started talking about intelligent algae. But what's so odd about that? Even the most complex life forms are just aggregations of individual cells working together. So if a few individual cells with rudimentary data-storage capacity got the idea of uniting why couldn't they act like a complex organism?

*   *   *   *   *

It is useless to speculate on what might have happened had that thing lived. But it's dead now— burned to death in acid. And although destruction of intelligent life is repugnant to me, I cannot help feeling that it is perhaps better that it is gone. Considering how rapidly it developed during its few weeks of life, and the power it possessed, my mind is appalled at its potential. I've had my experience and that's enough. Lord! but I'm tired. I feel like a wrung-out sponge. Guess I'll rest for a little while ...

... and received a reply to my signal! They heterodyned it right back along my own beam. They'll be landing in a week. I don't think I'll take this manuscript with me. I couldn't use it—and somehow I don't feel like burning it. Maybe I'll make a time capsule out of it. It will be amusing to speculate about what sort of a reaction it'll provoke, providing it is ever read. I can see them now, huge-headed humans, wrinkling their noses and saying "Intelligent algae—fantastic—the man must have been mad!"

The manuscript ends here—and of course we know that the "man" was not mad. He left behind a rich heritage indeed, for those few cells that escaped his wrath and floated down to the sea. Did we but know his origin we would erect a suitable memorial if we had to travel to the farthest reach of our galaxy. But the names he quotes are not in our repositories and as for the word "Earth" which he used for his homeworld, I need not remind my readers that the intelligent terrestrial inhabitants of the 22,748 planets of this sector use the term "Earth" or its synonyms "soil" and "world" to describe their planets. Of course, the term "Homewater" is gradually replacing this archaic concept as we extend our hegemony ever more widely across the disunited worlds of the galaxy.

At that it seems strange that the unknown author's race should have passed. As individuals they had so many advantages, while we are so weak and individually so helpless. They could do almost everything except communicate and cooperate. We can do but little else, yet our larger aggregations can control entire worlds, some peopled perhaps with descendants of this very individual. It merely proves that Dannar's statement in the preface of his Thesis is correct.

"United, cohesive cooperation is the source of irresistible strength."

It was a big joke on all concerned. When you look back, the whole thing really began because his father had a sense of humor. Oh, the name fit all right, but can you imagine naming your son....

NOBLE REDMAN

ILLUSTRATED BY GRAYAM
ORIGINALLY PUBLISHED IN
AMAZING SCIENCE FICTION STORIES
JULY 1960

Noble Redman

A pair of words I heartily detest are *noble* and *redman*, particularly when they occur together. Some of my egghead friends from the Hub tell me that I shouldn't, since they're merely an ancient colloquialism used to describe a race of aborigines on the American land mass.

The American land mass? Where? Why—on Earth, of course—where would ancestors come from? Yes—I know it's not nice to mention that word. It's an obscenity. No one likes to be reminded that his ancestors came from there. It's like calling a man a son of a sloat. But it's the truth. Our ancestors came from Earth and nothing we can do is going to change it. And despite the fact that we're the rulers of a good sized segment of the galaxy, we're nothing but transplanted Earthmen.

I suppose I'm no better than most of the citizens you find along the peripheral strips of Martian dome cities. But I might have been if it hadn't been for Noble Redman. No—not *the* noble redman—just Noble Redman. It's a name, not a description, although as a description his surname could apply, since he *was* red. His skin was red, his hair was red, his eyes had reddish flecks in their irises, and their whites were red like they were inflamed. Even his teeth had a reddish tinge. Damndest guy I ever saw. Redman was descriptive enough—but Noble! Ha! that character had all the nobility of a Sand Nan—.

I met him in Marsport. I was fairly well-heeled, having just finished guiding a couple Centaurian tourists through the ruins of K'nar. They didn't believe me when I told them to watch out for Sand Nans. Claimed that there were no such things. They were kinda violent about it. Superstition—they said. So when the Nan heaved itself up out of the sand, they weren't ready at all. They froze long enough for it to get in two shots with its stingers. They were paralyzed of course, but I wasn't, and a Nan isn't quick enough to hit a running target. So I was out of range when the Nan turned its attention to the Centaurians and started to feed. I took a few pictures of the Nan finishing off the second tourist— the female one. It wasn't very pretty, but you learn to keep a camera handy when you're a guide. It gets you out of all sorts of legal complications later. The real bad thing about it was that the woman must have gotten stuck with an unripe stinger because she didn't go quietly like her mate. She kept screaming right up to the end. I felt bad about it, but there wasn't anything I could do. You don't argue with a Nan without a blaster, and the Park Service doesn't allow weapons in Galactic Parks.

*   *   *   *   *

Despite the fact that I had our conversation on tape and pictures to prove what happened, the Park cops took a dim view of the whole affair. They cancelled my license, but what the hell—I wasn't cut out for a guide. So when I got back to Marsport, I put in a claim for my fee, and since their money had gone into the Nan with them, the Claims Court allowed that I had the right to garnishee the deceaseds' personal property, which I did. So I was richer by one Starflite class yacht, a couple of hundred ounces of industrial gold, and a lot of personal effects which I sold to Abe Feldstein for a hundred and fifty munits.

Abe wasn't very generous, but what's a Martian to do with Centaurian gear? Nothing those midgets use is adaptable to us. Even their yacht, a six passenger job, would barely hold three normal-sized people and they'd be cramped as kampas in a can. But the hull and drives were in good shape and I figured that if I sunk a couple of thousand munits into remodelling, the ship'd sell for at least twenty thousand—if I could find someone who wanted a three passenger job. That was the problem.

Abe offered me five thousand for her as she stood—but I wasn't having any—at least not until I'd gotten rid of the gold in her fuel reels. That stuff's worth money to the spacelines—about fifty munits per ounce. It's better even than lead as fuel—doesn't clog the tubes and gives better acceleration.

Well—like I said—I was flusher than I had been since Triworld Freight Lines ran afoul of the cops on Callisto for smuggling tekla nuts. So I went down to Otto's place on the strip to wash some of that Dryland dust off my tonsils. And that's where I met Redman.

He came up the street from the South airlock—a big fellow—walking kinda unsteady, his respirator hanging from his thick neck. He was burned a dark reddish black from the Dryland sun and looked like he was on his last legs when he turned into Otto's. He staggered up to the bar.

"Water," he said.

Otto passed him a pitcher and damned if the guy didn't drink it straight down!

"That'll be ten munits," Otto said.

"For water?" the man asked.

"You're on Mars," Otto reminded him.

"Oh," the big fellow said, and jerked a few lumps of yellow metal out of a pocket and dropped it on the bar. "Will this do?" he asked.

*   *   *   *   *

Otto's eyes damn near bulged out of their sockets. "Where'd you get that stuff?" he demanded. "That's gold!"

"I know."

"It'll do fine." Otto picked out a piece that musta weighed an ounce. "Have another pitcher."

"That's enough," the big fellow said. "Keep the change."

"Yes, sir!" You'da thought from Otto's voice that he was talking to the Prince Regent. "Just *where* did you say you found it."

"I didn't say. But I found it out there." He waved a thick arm in the direction of the Drylands.

By this time a couple of sharpies sitting at one of the tables pricked up their ears, removed their pants from their chairs and began closing in. But I beat them to it.

"My name's Wallingford," I said. "Cyril Wallingford."

"So what?" he snaps.

"So if you don't watch out you'll be laying in an alley with all that nice yellow stuff in someone else's pocket."

"I can take care of myself," he said.

"I don't doubt it," I said, looking at the mass of him. He was sure king-sized. "But even a guy as big as you is cold meat for a little guy with a Kelly."

He looked at me a bit more friendly. "Maybe I'm wrong about you, friend. But you look shifty."

"I'll admit my face isn't my fortune," I said sticking out what little chin I had and looking indignant. "But I'm honest. Ask anyone here." I looked around. There were three men in the place I didn't have something on, and I was faster than they. I was a fair hand with a Kelly in those days and I had a reputation. There was a chorus of nods and the big fellow looked satisfied. He stuck out a hamsized hand.

"Me name's Redman," he said. "Noble Redman. My father had a sense of humor." He grinned at me, giving me a good view of his pink teeth.

I grinned back. "Glad to know you," I replied. I gave the sharpies a hard look and they moved off and left us alone. The big fellow interested me. Fact is—anyone with money interested me—but I'm not stupid greedy. It took me about three minutes to spot him for a phony. Anyone who's lived out in the Drylands knows that there just *isn't* any gold there. Iron, sure, the whole desert's filthy with it, but if there is anything higher on the periodic table than the rare earths, nobody had found it yet—and

this guy with his light clothes, street boots and low
capacity respirator—Hell! he couldn't stay out there more
than two days if he wanted to—and besides, the gold was
refined. The lumps looked like they were cut off
something bigger—a bar, for instance.

*   *   *   *   *

A bar!—a bar of gold! My brain started working. K'nar
was about two days out, and there had always been
rumors about Martian gold even though no one ever
found any. Maybe this tourist had come through. If so, he
was worth cultivating. For he was a tourist. He certainly
wasn't a citizen. There wasn't a Martian alive with a skin
like his. Redman—the name fitted all right. But what
was his game? I couldn't figure it. And the more I tried
the less I succeeded. It was a certainty he was no
prospector despite his burned skin. His hands gave him
away. They were big and dirty, but the pink nails were
smooth and the red palms soft and uncalloused. There
wasn't even a blister on them. He could have been fresh
from the Mercury Penal Colony—but those guys were
burned black—not red, and he didn't have the hangdog
look of an ex-con.

He talked about prospecting on Callisto—looking for
heavy metals. Ha! There were fewer heavy metals on
Callisto than there were on Mars. But he had listeners.
His gold and the way he spent it drew them like honey
draws flies. But finally I got the idea. Somehow, subtly,
he turned the conversation around to gambling which
was a subject everyone knew. That brought up tales of
the old games, poker, faro, three card monte, blackjack,
roulette—and crapshooting.

"I'll bet there isn't a dice game in town." Redman said.

"You'd lose," I answered. I had about all this
maneuvering I could take. Bring it out in the open—see
what this guy was after. Maybe I could get something out
of it in the process. From the looks of his hands he was a

pro. He could probably make dice and cards sing sweet music, and if he could I wanted to be with him when he did. The more I listened, the more I was sure he was setting something up.

"Where is this game?" he asked incuriously.

"Over Abie Feldstein's hock-shop," I said. "But it's private. You have to know someone to get in."

"You steering for it?" He asked.

I shook my head, half puzzled. I wasn't quite certain what he meant.

"Are you touting for the game?" he asked.

The light dawned. But the terms he used! Archaic was the only word for them!

"No," I said, "I'm not fronting for Abie. Fact is, if you want some friendly advice, stay outa there."

"Why—the game crooked?"

There it was again, the old fashioned word. "Yes, it's bowed," I said. "It's bowed like a sine wave—in both directions. Honesty isn't one of Abie's best policies."

He suddenly looked eager. "Can I get in?" he asked.

"Not through me. I have no desire to watch a slaughter of the innocent. Hang onto your gold, Redman. It's safer." I kept watching him. His face smoothed out into an expressionless mask—a gambler's face. "But if you're really anxious, there's one of Abie's fronts just coming in the door. Ask him, if you want to lose your shirt."

"Thanks," Redman said.

I didn't wait to see what happened. I left Otto's and laid a courseline for Abie's. I wanted to be there before Redman arrived. Not only did I want an alibi, but I'd be in better position to sit in. Also I didn't want a couple of Abie's goons on my neck just in case Redman won. There was no better way to keep from getting old than to win too many munits in Abie's games.

*   *   *   *   *

I'd already given Abie back fifty of the hundred and fifty he'd paid me for the Centaurians' gear, and was starting in on the hundred when Redman walked in flanked by the frontman. He walked straight back to the dice table and stood beside it, watching the play. It was an oldstyle table built for six-faced dice, and operated on percentage—most of the time. It was a money-maker, which was the only reason Abie kept it. People liked these old-fashioned games. They were part of the Martian tradition. A couple of local citizens and a dozen tourists were crowded around it, and the diceman's flat emotionless voice carried across the intermittent click and rattle of the dice across the green cloth surface.

I dropped out of the blackjack game after dropping another five munits, and headed slowly towards the dice table. One of the floormen looked at me curiously since I didn't normally touch dice, but whatever he thought he kept to himself. I joined the crowd, and watched for awhile.

Redman was sitting in the game, betting at random. He played the field, come and don't come, and occasionally number combinations. When it came his turn at the dice he made two passes, a seven and a four the hard way, let the pile build and crapped out on the next roll. Then he lost the dice with a seven after an eight. There was nothing unusual about it, except that after one run of the table I noticed that he won more than he lost. He was pocketing most of his winnings—but I was watching him close and keeping count. That was enough for me. I got into the game, followed his lead, duplicating his bets. And I won too.

People are sensitive. Pretty quick they began to see that Redman and I were winning and started to follow our leads. I gave them a dirty look and dropped out, and after four straight losses, Redman did likewise.

He went over to the roulette wheel and played straight red and black. He won there too. And after awhile he went back to the dice table. I cashed in. Two thousand was fair enough and there was no reason to make myself unpopular. But I couldn't help staying to watch the fun. I could feel it coming—a sense of something impending.

Redman's face was flushed a dull vermilion, his eyes glittered with ruby glints, and his breath came faster. The dice had a grip on him just like cards do on me. He was a gambler all right—one of the fool kind that play it cozy until they're a little ahead and then plunge overboard and drown.

"Place your bets, ladies and gentlemen," the diceman droned. "Eight is the point." His rake swept over the board collecting a few munit plaques on the wrong spots. Redman had the dice. He rolled. Eight—a five and a three. "Let it ride," he said,—and I jumped nervously. He should have said, "Leave it." But the diceman was no purist. Another roll—seven. The diceman looked inquiringly at Redman. The big man shook his head, and rolled again—four. Three rolls later he made his point. Then he rolled another seven, another seven, and an eleven. And the pile of munits in front of him had become a respectable heap.

"One moment, sir," the diceman said as he raked in the dice. He rolled them in his hands, tossed them in the air, and handed them back.

"That's enough," Redman said. "Cash me in."

"But—"

"I said I had enough."

"Your privilege, sir."

"One more then," Redman said, taking the dice and stuffing munits into his jacket. He left a hundred on the board, rolled, and came up with a three. He grinned. "Thought I'd pushed my luck as far as it would go," he said, as he stuffed large denomination bills into his pockets.

*   *   *   *   *

I sidled up to him. "Get out of here, buster," I said. "That diceman switched dice on you. You're marked now."

"I saw him," Redman replied in a low voice, not looking at me. "He's not too clever, but I'll stick around, maybe try some more roulette."

"It's your funeral," I whispered through motionless lips.

He turned away and I left. There was no reason to stay, and our little talk just might have drawn attention. They could have a probe tuned on us now. I went down the strip to Otto's and waited. It couldn't have been more than a half hour later that Redman came by. He was looking over his shoulder and walking fast. His pockets, I noted, were bulging. So I went out the back door, cut down the serviceway to the next radius street, and flagged a cab.

"Where to, mister?" the jockey said.

"The strip—and hurry."

The jockey fed propane to the turbine and we took off like a scorched zarth. "Left or right?" he asked as the strip leaped at us. I crossed my fingers, estimated the speed of Redman's walk, and said, "Right."

We took the corner on two of our three wheels and there was Redman, walking fast toward the south airlock, and behind him, half-running, came two of Abie's goons.

"Slow down—*fast!*" I yapped, and was crushed against the back of the front seat as the jock slammed his foot on the brakes. "In here!" I yelled at Redman as I swung the rear door open.

His reflexes were good. He hit the floor in a flat dive as the purple streak of a stat blast flashed through the space where he had been. The jockey needed no further stimulation. He slammed his foot down and we took off with a screech of polyprene, whipped around the next corner and headed for the hub, the cops, and safety.

"Figured you was jerking some guy, Cyril," the jockey said over his shoulder. "But who is he?"

*   *   *   *   *

Redman picked himself off the floor as I swore under my breath. The jockey *would* have to know me. Abie'd hear of my part in this by morning and my hide wouldn't be worth the price of a mangy rat skin. I had to get out of town—fast! And put plenty of distance between me and Marsport. This dome—this planet—wasn't going to be healthy for quite a while. Abie was the most unforgiving man I knew where money was concerned, and if the large, coarse notes dripping from Redman's pockets were any indication, there was lots of money concerned.

"Where to now, Cyril?" the jockey asked.

There was only one place to go. I damned the greed that made me pick Redman up. I figured that he'd be grateful to the tune of a couple of kilomunits but what was a couple of thousand if Abie thought I was mixed up in this? Lucky I had a spaceship even if she was an unconverted Centaurian. I could stand the cramped quarters a lot better than I could take a session in Abie's back room. I'd seen what happened to guys who went in there, and it wasn't pretty. "To the spaceport," I said, "and don't spare the hydrocarbons."

"Gotcha!" the jock said and the whine of the turbine increased another ten decibels.

"Thanks, Wallingford," Redman said. "If you hadn't pulled me out I'd have had to shoot somebody. And I don't like killing. It brings too many lawmen into the picture." He was as cool as ice. I had to admire his nerve.

"Thanks for nothing," I said. "I figured you'd be grateful in a more solid manner."

"Like this?" he thrust a handful of bills at me. There must have been four thousand in that wad. It cheered me up a little.

"Tell me where you want to get off," I said.

"You said you have a spaceship," he countered.

"I do, but it's a Centaurian job. I might be able to squeeze into it but I doubt if you could. About the only spot big enough for you would be the cargo hold, and the radiation'd fry you before we even made Venus."

He grinned at me. "I'll take the chance," he said.

"Okay, sucker," I thought. "You've been warned." If he came along he'd damn well go in the hold. I could cut the drives after we got clear of Mars and dump him out— after removing his money, of course. "Well," I said aloud, "it's your funeral."

"You're always saying that," he said with chuckle in his voice.

*   *   *   *   *

We checked out at the airlock and drove out to the spaceport over the sand-filled roadbed that no amount of work ever kept clean. We cleared the port office, drew spacesuits from Post Supply, and went out to my yacht. Redman looked at her, his heart in his eyes. He seemed overwhelmed by it.

"Lord! she's beautiful!" he breathed, as he looked at the slim polished length standing on her broad fins, nose pointed skyward.

"Just a Starflite-class yacht," I said.

"Look, Cyril," he said. "Will you sell her?"

"If we get to Venus alive and you still want to buy her, she'll cost you—" I hesitated, "twenty-five thousand."

"Done!" he said. It came so fast that I figured I should have asked for fifty.

"The fuel will be extra," I said. "Fifty munits an ounce. There's maybe ten pounds of it."

"How far will that take me?"

"About ten light-years at cruising speed. Gold is economical."

"That should be far enough," he said with a faint smile.

We drew the boarding ladder down and prepared to squeeze aboard. As I figured it, we had plenty of time, but I hadn't counted on that nosy guard at the check station,

or maybe that character at the south airlock of the dome,
because I was barely halfway up the ladder to the hatch
when I heard the howl of a racing turbine and two
headlights came cutting through the night over the
nearest dune. The speed with which that car was coming
argued no good.

"Let's go," I said, making with the feet.

"I'm right behind you," Redman said into my left heel.
"Hurry! Those guys are out for blood!"

I tumbled through the lock and wiggled up the narrow
passageway. By some contortionist's trick Redman came
through the hatch feet first, an odd looking gun in his
hand. Below us the turbo screeched to a stop and men
boiled out, blasters in hand. They didn't wait—just
started firing. Electrostatic discharges leaped from the
metal of the ship, but they were in too much of a hurry.
The gun in Redman's fist steadied as he took careful aim.
A tiny red streak hissed out of the muzzle—and the roof
fell in! A thunderous explosion and an eye-wrenching
burst of light filled the passageway through the slit in the
rapidly closing hatch. The yacht rocked on her base like a
tree in a gale, as the hatch slammed shut.

"What in hell was *that*?" I yelped.

"Just a low yield nuclear blast," Redman said. "About
two tons. Those lads won't bother us any more."

"You fool!—you stupid moronic abysmal fool!" I said
dully. "You're not content to get Abie on our heels. Now
you've triggered off the whole Galactic Patrol. Don't you
know that nuclear weapons are banned—that they've
been banned ever since our ancestors destroyed Earth—
that their use calls for the execution of the user? Just
where do you come from that you don't know the facts of
life?"

"Earth," Redman said.

*   *   *   *   *

It left me numb. Any fool knew that there was no life on that radioactive hell. Even now, spacers could see her Van Allen bands burning with blue-green fire. Earth was a sterile world—a horrible example, the only forbidden planet in the entire galaxy, a galactic chamber of horrors ringed with automatic beacons and patrol ships to warn strangers off. We Martians, Earth's nearest neighbor, had the whole history of that last suicidal war drummed into us as children. After all, we *were* the cradle of Galactic civilization even though we got that way by being driven off Earth—and feeling that almost any place would be better than Mars. Mars iron built the ships and powered the atomics that had conquered the galaxy. But we knew Earth better than most, and to hear those words from Redman's lips was a shock.

"You're a damn liar!" I exploded.

"You're entitled to your opinion," Redman said, "but you should know the truth when it is told to you. I *am* from Earth!"

"But—" I said.

"You'd better get out of here," Redman said, "your Patrol will be here shortly."

I was thinking that, too. So I wiggled my way up to the control room, braced myself against the walls and fired the jets. Acceleration crushed me flat as the ship lifted and bored out into space.

As quickly as I could, I cut the jets so the Patrol couldn't trace us by our ion trail, flipped the negative inertia generator on and gave the ship one minimal blast that hurled her out of sight. We coasted at a few thousand miles per second along the plane of the ecliptic while we took stock.

Redman had wedged himself halfway into the control room and eyed my cramped body curiously. "It's a good thing you're a runt," he said. "Otherwise we'd be stuck down there." He laughed. "You look like a jack in the box—all coiled up ready to spring out."

But I was in no mood for humor. Somehow I felt that I'd been conned. "What do I get out of this?" I demanded.

"A whole skin—at least for awhile."

"That won't do me any good unless I can take it somewhere."

"Don't worry," Redman said. "They don't give a damn about you. It's me they want, turn on your radio and see."

I flipped the switch and a voice came into the control room—"remind you that this is a Galactic emergency! The Patrol has announced that an inhabitant of Earth has been on Mars! This individual is dangerously radioactive. A reward of one hundred thousand Galactic munits will be paid to the person who gives information leading to his death or capture. I repeat,—*one hundred thousand munits*! The man's description is as follows: Height 180 centimeters, weight 92 kilograms, eyes reddish brown, hair red. A peculiarity which makes him easily recognized is the red color of his skin. He is armed with a nuclear weapon and is dangerous. When last seen he was leaving Marsport spacefield. Starflite class yacht, registration number CY 127439. He has a citizen with him, probably a hostage. If seen, notify the nearest Patrol ship."

*   *   *   *   *

I looked at Redman. The greed must have shone from me like a beacon. "A hundred grand!" I said softly.

"Try and collect," Redman said.

"I'm not going to," I said and turned three separate plans to capture him over in my head.

"They won't work," Redman said. He grinned nastily. "And don't worry about radioactivity. I'm no more contaminated than you are."

"Yeah?—and just how do you live on that hotbox without being contaminated?" I asked.

"Simple. The surface isn't too hot in the first place. Most of the stuff is in the Van Allen belts. Second, we live underground. And third we're protected."

"How?"

"Where do you think this red skin comes from? It isn't natural. Even you should know that. Actually we had the answer to protection during the Crazy Years before the blowup when everybody talked peace and built missiles. A bacteriologist named Anderson discovered it while working with radiation sterilized food. He isolated a whole family of bacteria from the food that not only survived, but lived normally in the presence of heavy doses of radiation. The microbes all had one thing in common—a peculiar reddish pigment that protected them.

"Luckily, the military of his nation—the United States, I think they called it, thought that this pigment might be a useful protective shield for supplies. Extracts were made and tested before the Blowup came, and there was quite a bit of it on hand.

"But the real hero of protection was a general named Ardleigh. He ordered every man and woman in his command inoculated with the extract right after the Blowup—when communications were disorganized and commanders of isolated units had unchallengeable power. He was later found to be insane, but his crazy idea was right. The inoculations killed ten per cent of his command and turned those who lived a bright red, but none of the living showed a sign of radiation sickness after they received the extract.

"By this time your ancestors—the Runners—had gone, and those who stayed were too busy trying to remain alive to worry much about them. The "Double A" vaccine—named for Anderson and Ardleigh—was given to every person and animal that could be reached, but it was only a small fraction of the population that survived. The others died. But enough men and animals remained to get a toe-hold on their ruined world, and they slowly rebuilt.

"We had forgotten about you Runners—but it seems you didn't forget us. You sealed us off—forced us to remain on Earth. And by the time we were again ready for space, you were able to prevent us. But we will not be denied forever. It took an entire planet working together to get me on Mars to learn your secrets. And when I got here, I found that I wouldn't have time to learn. We had forgotten one simple thing—my skin color. It isn't normal here and there is no way of changing it since the extract combines permanently with body cells. So I had to do the next best thing—obtain a sample of your technology and bring it to Earth. I planned at first to get enough money to buy a ship. But those creeps in Marsport don't lose like gentlemen. I damn near had to beat my way out of that joint. And when a couple of them came after me, I figured it was all up. I could kill them of course, but that wouldn't solve anything. Since I can't fly one of your ships yet, I couldn't steal one—and I wouldn't have time to buy one because I was pretty sure the Patrol would be after me as soon as the rumors of a red man got around. You see— *they* know what we look like and its their job to keep us cooped up—"

"Hmm," I said.

"Why do they do it?" Redman asked. "We're just as human as you are." He shrugged. "At any rate," he finished, "I was at the end of my rope when you came along. But you have a ship—you can fly—and you'll take me back to Earth."

"I will?" I asked.

*   *   *   *   *

He nodded. "I can make it worth your while," he said.

"How?" I asked.

"Money. You'll do anything for money." Redman looked at me soberly. "You're a repulsive little weasel, Cyril, and I would distrust you thoroughly except that I know you as well as you know me. That's the virtue of being human. We understand each other without words. You are a cheap, chiseling, doublecrossing, money-grabbing heel. You'd kick your mother's teeth out for a price. And for what I'm going to offer you, you'll jump at the chance to help us—but I don't have to tell you that. You know already."

"What do you mean—know already?" I said. "Can I read your mind?"

"Do you mean to tell me—" Redman began. And then a peculiar smile crossed his face, a light of dawning comprehension. "Why no," he said, "why should you be telepathic—why should you? And to think I kept hiding—" he broke off and looked at me with a superior look a man gives his dog. Affectionate but pitying. "No wonder there were no psych fields protecting that dice game—and I thought—" he started to laugh.

*   *   *   *   *

And I knew then why the Patrol had sealed Earth off. Mutated by radiation, speeded up in their evolution by the effects of the Blowup, Earthmen were as far ahead of us mentally as we were ahead of them technologically. To let these telepaths, these telekinetics—and God knows what else—loose on the Galaxy would be like turning a bunch of hungry kelats loose in a herd of fat sloats. My head buzzed like it was filled with a hive of bees. For the first time in years I stopped thinking of the main chance. So help me, I was feeling *noble*!

"Just take it easy, Cyril," Redman said. "Don't get any bright ideas."

Bright ideas! Ha! I should be getting bright ideas with a character who could read me like a book. What I needed was something else.

"If you cooperate," Redman said, "you'll be fixed for life."

"You're not kidding," I said. "I'd be fixed all right. The Patrol'd hound me all the way to Andromeda if I helped you. And don't think they wouldn't find out. While we can't read minds, we can tell when a man's lying."

"Have you ever heard of Fort Knox?" Redman asked.

Fort Knox—Fort Knox—*fourknocks*! the thought staggered me.

"The gold I had came from there," Redman said.

Fourknocks! Sure, I'd heard of it. What citizen hadn't? They still tell stories of that fabulous hoard of gold. Tons of it buried on Earth waiting for someone with guts enough to go in and find it.

"All your ship will hold," Redman said. "After we analyze its principles."

Five tons of gold! Six million munits! So much money! It staggered me. I'd never dreamed of that much money. Redman was right. I *would* kick my mother's teeth out if the price was right. And the price—I jumped convulsively. My arm brushed the control board, kicking off the negative inertia and slapping the axial correction jets.

The ship spun like a top! Centrifugal force crushed me against the control room floor. Redman, an expression of pained surprise on his face before it slammed against the floor, was jammed helplessly in the corridor. I had time for one brief grin. The Patrol would zero in on us, and I'd have a hundred thousand I could spend. What could I do with six million I couldn't use?

Then hell broke out. A fire extinguisher came loose from its fastenings and started flying around the room in complete defiance of artificial gravity. Switches on the control board clicked on and off. The ship bucked, shuddered and jumped. But the spin held. Redman, crushed face down to the floor, couldn't see what he was doing. Besides—he didn't know what he was doing—but he was trying. The fire extinguisher came whizzing across the floor and cracked me on the shin. A scream of pure agony left my lips as I felt the bone snap.

"Got you!" Redman grunted, as he lifted his head against the crushing force and sighted at me like a gunner. The extinguisher reversed its flight across the room and came hurtling at my head.

"Too late!" I gloated mentally. Then the world was filled with novae and comets as the extinguisher struck. The cheerful thought that Redman was trapped because he didn't—couldn't—know how to drive a hypership was drowned in a rush of darkness.

* * * * *

When I came to, my leg was aching like a thousand devils and I was lying on a rocky surface. Near—terribly near—was a jagged rock horizon cutting the black of space dotted with the blazing lights of stars. I groaned and rolled over, wincing at the double pain in leg and head. Redman was standing over me, carrying a couple of oxygen bottles and a black case. He looked odd, standing there with a load in his arms that would have crushed him flat on Mars. And then I knew. I was on an asteroid.

"But how did I get here?"

"Easy," Redman's voice came over my headphone. "Didn't anyone ever tell you an unconscious mind is easier to read than a conscious one?" He chuckled. "No," he continued, "I don't suppose they did—but it is. Indeed it is." He laid the bottles down, and put the box beside them. "I learned how to operate the ship, stopped the spin, and got her back into negative inertia before the Patrol found me. Found this place about an hour ago— and since you began to look like you'd live, I figured you should have a chance. So I'm leaving you a communicator and enough air to keep you alive until you can get help. But so help me—you don't deserve it. After I played square with you, you try to do this to me."

"Square!" I yelped. "Why you—" The rest of what I said was unprintable.

Redman grinned at me, his face rosy behind the glassite of his helmet—and turned away. I turned to watch him picking his way carefully back to where the yacht rested lightly on the naked rock. At the airlock he turned and waved at me. Then he squeezed inside. The

lock closed. There was a brief shimmer around the ship—
a briefer blast of heat, and the yacht vanished.

I turned on the communicator and called for help. I
used the Patrol band. "I'll keep the transmitter turned on
so you can home in on me," I broad-casted, "but get that
Earthman first! He's got my money and my ship. Pick me
up later, but get him now!"

I didn't know whether my message was received or
not, because Redman didn't leave me any receiver other
than the spacesuit intercom in my helmet. It was, I
suspected, a deliberate piece of meanness on his part. So I
kept talking until my voice was a hoarse croak, calling
the Patrol, calling—calling—calling, until a black shark
shape blotted out the stars overhead and a couple of
Patrolmen in jetsuits homed in on me.

"Did you get him?" I asked.

The Patrolman bending over me shrugged his
shoulders. "They haven't told me," he said.

*   *   *   *   *

They hauled me back to Marsport, put my leg in a
cast, ran me through the lie detector, and then tossed me
in jail for safekeeping. I beefed about the jail, but not too
loud. As I figured it I was lucky to be out of Abie's hands.

Two days later, a Patrolman with the insignia of a
Commander on his collar tabs showed up at my cell. He
was apologetic. I was a hero, he said. Seems like the
Patrol caught Redman trying to sneak through the
asteroid belt on standard drive and blasted him out of
space.

So they gave me the reward and turned me loose.

But it didn't do me any good. After taxes, it only came
to twenty thousand, and Abie grabbed that before I could
get out of town. Like I said, Abie's unforgiving where
money's concerned, and Redman had taken him for over
thirty kilos, which, according to Abie was my fault for
lifting him and getting him out of town. After he got my

twenty kilos he still figured I owed him twelve—and so I've never made it back. Every time I get a stake he grabs it, and what with the interest, I still owe him twelve.

But I still keep trying, because there's still a chance. You see, when Redman probed around in my mind to learn how to run the spaceship, he was in a hurry. He must have done something to my brain, because when he left me on that asteroid, as he turned and waved at me, I could hear him thinking that the Patrol would not be able to stop hyperships, and if he made it to Earth his people could emigrate to some clean world and stop having to inject their kids, and while they couldn't make the grade themselves, their kids could crash the Galaxy without any trouble. I got the impression that it wouldn't be too much trouble to empty Earth. Seems as though there wasn't many more than a million people left. The red color wasn't complete protection apparently.

And there's another thing. About a month after I got the reward, there was a minor complaint from Centaurus V about one of their officials who disappeared on a vacation trip to Mars. His ship was a Starflite class, Serial CY 122439. Get the idea?

So I keep watching all the incoming tourists like you. Someday I figure I'm going to run into a decolorized Earthman. They won't be able to stay away any more than the other peoples of the Galaxy. Old Mother Earth keeps dragging them back even though they've been gone for over a thousand years. Don't get the idea they want to see Mars. It's Earth that draws them. And it'll draw an Earthman's kids. And I figure that if I could read Redman's mind, I can read theirs, too even though I haven't read a thought since. It figures, does it not?

Hey! Hold on! There's no need to run. All I want to do is collect a fifty year old bill—plus interest. Your folks owe me that much.

᛫

To Choke an Ocean

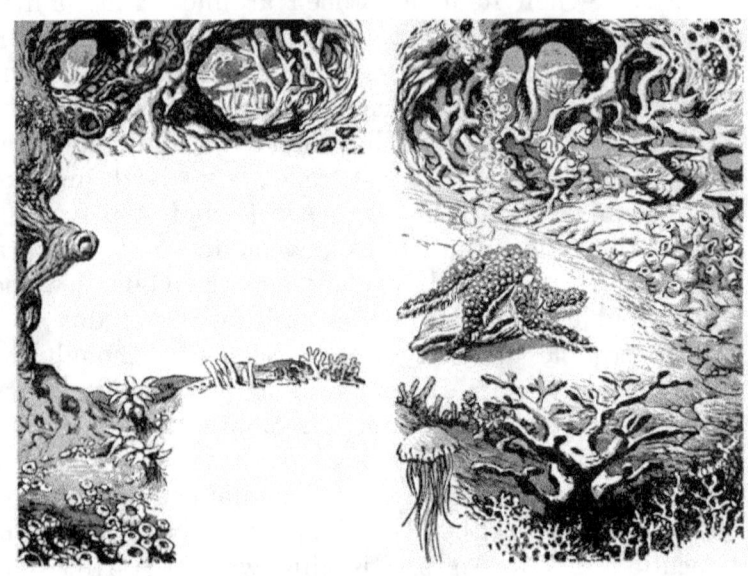

ILLUSTRATED BY WOOD
ORIGINALLY PUBLISHED IN IF WORLDS OF SCIENCE FICTION
SEPTEMBER, 1960

*Gourmets all agree that nothing can beat oysters
on the half-shell—
not even the armed might of the Terran Confederation!*

To Choke an Ocean

"Nice that you dropped in," the man in the detention room said. "I never expected a visit from the Consul General. It makes me feel important."

"The Confederation takes an interest in all of its citizens' welfare," Lanceford said. "You *are* important! Incidentally, how is it going?"

"Not too bad. They treat me all right. But these natives sure are tough on visitors. I've never been checked so thoroughly in all my life—and now this thirty day quarantine! Why, you'd think I was carrying the plague instead of a sample case!"

The chubby little commercial traveller probably had a right to complain, Lanceford thought. After all, a Niobian quarantine station isn't the pleasantest sort of environment. It's not meant to be comfortable, physical discomfort being as good a way as any to discourage casual visitors. The ones who have fortitude enough to stand the entry regulations can get in, but tourists seldom visit Niobe. However, the planet's expanding economy offered a fertile field for salesmen, and men of that stripe would endure far worse hardships than a port of entry in pursuit of the Almighty Credit.

Now this fellow, George Perkins, was a typical salesman. And despite his soft exterior there was a good hard core inside.

Lanceford looked him over and decided that he would last. "You came here of your own free will, didn't you?" he asked.

"If you call a company directive free will," Perkins answered. "I wouldn't come here for a vacation, if that's what you mean. But the commercial opportunities can't be ignored."

"I suppose not, but you can hardly blame the Niobians for being suspicious of strangers. Perhaps there's no harm in you. But they have a right to be sure; they've been burned before." Lanceford uncoiled his lean gray length from the chair and walked over to the broad armorglas window. He stared out at the gloomy view of Niobe's rainswept polar landscape. "You know," he continued, "you might call this Customs Service a natural consequence of uninvestigated visitors." He brooded over the grayness outside. A polar view was depressing— scrubby vegetation, dank grassland, the eternal Niobian rain. He felt sorry for Perkins. Thirty days in this place would be sheer torture.

"It must have been quite some disturbance to result in this." Perkins waved his hand at the barren room. "Sounds like you know something about it."

"I do. In a way you might say that I was responsible for it."

"Would you mind telling me?"

*   *   *   *   *

"I wouldn't mind at all." Lanceford looked at his watch. "If I have the time, that is. I'm due to be picked up in an hour, but Niobians have some quaint conceptions of time. So if you want to take a chance that I won't finish—"

"Go ahead."

"To start with, take a look at that insigne over the door. The whole story's right there."

Perkins eyed the emblem of the Niobian Customs Service. It was a five-pointed star surrounding a circle, superimposed over the typically Terran motto: "Eternal Vigilance is the Price of Safety." He nodded.

"How come the Terran style?" he asked.

"That's part of the story. Actually that insigne's a whole chapter of Niobe's history. But you have to know what it stands for." Lanceford sighed reminiscently. "It began during the banquet that celebrated the signing of the Agreement which made Niobe a member of the Confederation. I was the Director of the BEE's Niobe Division at that time. As a matter of fact, I'd just taken the job over from Alvord Sims. The Old Man had been ordered back to Terra, to take over a job in the Administration, and I was the next man in line.

"The banquet was a flop, of course. Like most mixed gatherings involving different races, it was a compromise affair. Nobody was satisfied. It dragged along in a spirit of suffering resignation—the Niobians quietly enduring the tasteless quality of the food, while the Confederation representatives, wearing unobtrusive nose plugs, suffered politely through the watered-down aroma and taste of the Niobian delicacies. All things being considered, it was moving along more smoothly than it had any right to, and if some moron on the kitchen staff hadn't used tobasco sauce instead of catsup, we'd probably have signed the Agreement and gone on happily ever after.

"But it didn't work out that way.

"Of course it wasn't entirely the kitchen's fault. There had to be some damn fool at the banquet who'd place the bomb where it would do some good. And of course I had to be it." Lanceford grinned. "About the only thing I have to say in my defense is that I didn't know it was loaded!"

Perkins looked at him expectantly as Lanceford paused. "Well, don't stop there," he said. "You've got me interested."

Lanceford smiled good-naturedly and went on.

* * * * *

We held the banquet in the central plaza of Base Alpha. It was the only roofed area on the planet large enough to hold the crowd of high brass that had assembled for the occasion. We don't do things that way now, but fifty years ago we had a lot to learn. In those days, the admission of a humanoid planet into the

Confederation was quite an event. The VIP's thought that the native population should be aware of it.

I was sitting between Kron Avar and one of the high brass from the Bureau of Interstellar Trade, a fellow named Hartmann. I had no business being in that rarefied air, since Kron was one of the two First Councilors and Hartmann ranked me by a couple of thousand files on the promotion list. But I happened to be a friend of Kron's, so protocol got stretched a bit in the name of friendship. He and I had been through a lot together when I was a junior explorer with the BEE some ten years before. We'd kept contact with each other ever since. We had both come up the ladder quite a ways, but a Planetary Director, by rights, belonged farther down the table. So there I was, the recipient of one of the places of honor and a lot of dirty looks.

Hartmann didn't think much of being bumped one seat away from the top. He wasn't used to associating with mere directors, and besides, I kept him from talking with Kron about trade relations. Kron was busy rehashing the old days when we were opening Niobe to viscayaculture. Trade didn't interest him very much, and Hartmann interested him less. Niobians are never too cordial to strangers, and he had never seen the BIT man before this meeting.

Anyway, the talk got around to the time he introduced me to vorkum, a native dish that acts as a systemic insect repellant—and tastes like one! And right then I got the bright idea that nearly wrecked Niobe.

As I said, there was both Niobian and Confederation food at the banquet, so I figured that it was a good time as any to get revenge for what my dog-headed friend did to my stomach a good decade before.

So I introduced him to Terran cooking.

Niobians assimilate it all right, but their sense of taste isn't the same as ours. Our best dishes are just mush to their palates, which are conditioned to sauces that would make the most confirmed spice lover on Earth run screaming for the water tap. They have a sense of the delicate, too, but it needs to be stimulated with something like liquid fire before they can appreciate it. For instance, Kron liked Earth peaches, but he spiced them with horseradish and red pepper.

I must admit that he was a good sport. He took the hors d'oeuvres in stride, swallowing such tasteless things as caviar, Roquefort and anchovy paste without so much as a grimace. Of course, I was taking an unfair advantage of Kron's natural courtesy, but it didn't bother me too much. He had rubbed that vorkum episode in for years. It was nice to watch him squirm.

When I pressed him to try an oyster cocktail, I figured things had gone far enough.

He took it, of course, even though anyone who knew Niobians could see that he didn't want any part of it. There was a pleading look in his eye that I couldn't ignore. After all, Kron was a friend. I was actually about to stop him when he pulled an oyster from its red bath and popped it into his mouth. There was a 'you'll be sorry' look on his face. I gestured to a waiter to remove the cocktail as he bit into the oyster, figuring, somewhat belatedly, that I had gone too far.

The grateful look I got from him was sufficient reward. But then it happened. Kron stopped looking grateful and literally snatched the cocktail back from the startled waiter!

He looked at me with an expression of disgust. "The first decent food thus far," he said, "and you attempt to send it away!"

"Huh?" I exclaimed stupidly. "I didn't want to make you miserable."

"Miserable! Hah! This dish is wonderful! What in the name of my First Ancestor is it?" His pleased grin was enough like a snarl to make Hartmann cringe in his chair. Since Kron and I were both speaking Niobian rather than Confed, he didn't understand what was happening. I suppose he thought that Kron was about to rip my throat out. It was a natural error, of course. You've seen a dog smile, and wondered what was going on behind the teeth? Well, Kron looked something like that. A Niobian with his dog-headed humanoid body is impressive under any conditions. When he smiles he can be downright frightening.

I winked at Hartmann. "Don't worry, sir," I said. "Everything's all right."

"It certainly is," Kron said in Confed. "This dish is delicious. Incidentally, friend Lanceford, what is it? It tastes something like our Komal, but with a subtle difference of flavor that is indescribable!"

"It's called an oyster cocktail, Kron," I said.

"This is a product of your world we would enjoy!" Kron said. "Although the sauce is somewhat mild, the flavor of the meat is exquisite!" He closed his eyes, savoring the taste. "It would be somewhat better with vanka," he said musingly. "Or perhaps with Kala berries."

I shuddered. I had tried those sauces once. Once was enough! I could still feel the fire.

"I wonder if you could ship them to us," Kron continued.

Hartmann's ears pricked up at the word "ship." It looked like an opening gambit for a fast sales talk on behalf of interstellar trade, a subject dear to his heart.

But I was puzzled. I couldn't figure it out until I tried one of the oysters—after which I knew! Some fool had dished them up in straight tobasco sauce! It took some time before I could talk, what with trying to wash the fire out of my mouth, and during the conversational hiatus Hartmann picked up the ball where I dropped it. So I sat by and listened, my burned mouth being in no condition for use.

*   *   *   *   *

"I'm afraid that we couldn't ship them," Hartmann said. "At least not on a commercial basis. Interstellar freight costs are prohibitive where food is concerned."

Kron nodded sadly. He passed the oysters to Tovan Harl, his fellow First Councilor. Harl went through the same reaction pattern Kron had shown.

"However," Hartmann continued, "we could send you a few dozen. Perhaps you could start a small oyster farm."

"Is this a plant?" Kron asked curiously.

"No, it's a marine animal with a hard outer shell."

"Just like our Komal. We could try planting some of them in our oceans. If they grow, we will be very obliged to you Terrans for giving us a new taste sensation."

"Since my tribe is a seafaring one," Harl interjected, "they can be raised under my supervision until we find the exact methods to propagate them in our seas."

Hartmann must have been happy to get off the hook. It was a small request, one that was easy to fulfill. It was a good thing that the Niobians didn't realize what concessions they could wring from the BIT. The Confederation had sunk billions into Niobe and was prepared to sink many more if necessary. They would go to almost any lengths to keep the natives happy. If that meant star-freighter loads of oysters, then it would be star-freighter loads of oysters. The Confederation needed the gerontin that grew on Niobe.

The commercial worlds needed the anti-aging drug more and more as the exploration of space continued—not to mention the popular demand. Niobe was an ideal herbarium for growing the swampland plant from which the complex of alkaloids was extracted.

So Hartmann made a note of it, and the subject was dropped.

I didn't think anything more about it. Kron was happy, Harl was happy, and Hartmann was feeling pleased with himself. There was no reason to keep the oyster question alive.

But it didn't die there. By some sort of telepathy the Niobians scattered along the long tables found out what had been getting talked about at the upper end.

By this time I was on the ball again. When the orders went in I slipped a note to the cooks to use tabasco or vanaka on the Niobian orders. It was fortunate that there was an ample supply of oysters available, because the banquet dissolved shortly thereafter into an outright oyster feed. The Niobians dropped all pretense. They wanted oysters—with vanaka, with tabasco or with Kala berries. The more effete Earth preparations didn't rouse the slightest enthusiasm, but the bivalve found its place in the hearts and stomachs of the natives. The oysters ultimately ran out, but one thing was certain. There was a definite bond of affection between our two utterly dissimilar species.

The era of good feeling persisted for several hours. There was no more quiet undertone of polite suffering among our guests. They were enjoying themselves. The Agreement was signed with hardly an exception being taken to its clauses and wording.

Niobe became a full member of the Confederation, with sovereign planetary rights, and the viscaya concentrate began flowing aboard the ships waiting at the polar bases.

A day later I got orders to start winding up the BEE's installations on Niobe. The consular service would take over after I had finished....

*   *   *   *   *

Lanceford looked at his watch. "Well, we're going to have time. It looks like they'll be late. Want to hear the rest of it?"

"Naturally," Perkins said. "I certainly wouldn't want you to stop here."

"Well," Lanceford continued, "the next four years weren't much."

*   *   *   *   *

We spent most of the time closing down the outpost and regional installations, but it took longer than I expected what with the difficulty in getting shipping space to move anything but viscaya concentrate off the planet. Of course, like any of the Confederation bureaus, the BEE died hard. With one thing and another, there were still a lot of our old people left. We still had the three main bases on the continental land masses in operating condition, plus a few regional experiment stations on Alpha Continent and the Marine Biology Labs on Varnel Island. I'd just closed the last regional stations on Beta and Gamma when Heinz Bergdorf paid me an official call.

Heinz was the senior biologist on Varnel. He was a good looking lad of Teutonic ancestry, one of those big blond kids who fool you. He didn't look like a scientist, but his skull held more knowledge of Niobe's oceans than was good for a man. He would have to unlearn a lot of it before he took his next job, or so I thought at the time.

Anyway, Heinz came into my office looking like someone had stolen his favorite fishnet. The expression of Olympian gloom on his beak-nosed face would have done credit to Zeus. It didn't take any great amount of brains to see that Heinz was worried. It stuck out all over him. He draped himself limply in the chair beside my desk.

"We've got troubles, Chief," he announced.

I grinned at him. I knew perfectly well why he was here. Something had come up that was too big for him to handle. That was Heinz's only fault, a belief in the omnipotence of higher authority. If he couldn't handle it, it was a certainty that I could—even though I knew nothing of either his specialty or his problems. However, I liked the man. I did my best to give him the fatherly advice he occasionally needed, although he would have been better off half the time if he hadn't taken it.

"Well, what's the trouble now?" I asked. "From the look on your face it must be unpleasant. Or maybe you're just suffering from indigestion."

"It's not indigestion, Chief."

"Well, don't keep me in suspense. Tell me so I can worry too."

I didn't like the way he looked. Of course, I'd been expecting trouble for the past year. Things had been going far too smoothly.

"Oysters!" Bergdorf said laconically.

"Oysters?"

I looked at him incredulously. Bergdorf sat straight up in his chair and faced me. There was no humor in his eyes. "For God's sake! You frightened me for a moment. You're joking, I hope."

"Far from it," Bergdorf replied. "I said oysters and I mean oysters. It's no joke! Just who was the unutterable idiot who planted them here?"

It took a minute before I remembered. "Hartmann," I said. "Of the BIT. He ordered them delivered at the request of Kron Avar and Tovan Harl. I suppose Harl planted them. I never paid very much attention to it."

"You should have. It would have been better if they had imported Bengal tigers! How long ago did this infernal insanity happen?"

"Right after the Agreement was signed, I guess. I'm sure it was no earlier than that, because Niobians met up with oysters for the first time at that affair." I still didn't get it, but there was no doubt that Heinz was serious. I tried to remember something about oysters, but other than the fact that they were good to eat and produced pearls I could think of nothing. Yet Bergdorf looked like the end of the world was at hand. There was something here that didn't add up. "Well, get on with it," I said. "As far as marine biology is concerned I'm as innocent as a Lyranian virgin. Tell me—what's wrong with the oysters?"

"Nothing! That's the trouble. They're nice healthy specimens of terrestrial *Ostrea lurida.* We found a floating limb with about a dozen spat clinging to it."

"Spat?"

"Immature oysters."

"Oh. Is that bad?"

"Sure it's bad. I suppose I'd better explain," Bergdorf said. "On Earth an oyster wouldn't be anything to worry about, even though it produces somewhere between sixteen and sixty million fertile eggs every year. On Earth this tremendous fertility is necessary for survival, but here on Niobe where there are no natural enemies to speak of, it's absolutely deadly!

"Just take these dozen spat we found. Year after next, they'd be breeding size, and would produce about three hundred million larvae. If everything went right, some three years later those three hundred million would produce *nine thousand trillion* baby oysters! Can you image how much territory nine thousand trillion oysters would cover?"

I stopped listening right then, and started looking at the map of Niobe pinned on the wall. "Good Lord! They'd cover the whole eastern seaboard of Alpha from pole to pole."

Bergdorf said smugly, "Actually, you're a bit over on your guess. Considering the short free swimming stage of the larvae, the slow eastern seaboard currents, poor bottom conditions and overcrowding, I doubt if they would cover more than a thousand miles of coastline by the fourth year. Most of them would die from environmental pressures.

"But that isn't the real trouble. Niobe's oceans aren't like Earth's. They're shallow. It's a rare spot that's over forty fathoms deep. As a result, oysters can grow almost anywhere. And that's what'll happen if they aren't stopped. Inside of two decades they'll destroy this world!"

"You're being an alarmist," I said.

"Not so much as you might think. I don't suppose that the oysters will invade dry land and chase the natives from one rain puddle to another, but they'll grow without check, build oyster reefs that'll menace navigation, change the chemical composition of Niobe's oceans, pollute the water with organic debris of their rotting bodies, and so change the ecological environment of this world that only the hardiest and most adaptable life forms will be able to survive this!"

"But they'll be self-limiting," I protested.

"Sure. But by the time they limit themselves, they will eliminate about everything else."

"If you're right, then, there's only one thing to do. We'll have to let the natives know what the score is and start taking steps to get rid of them."

"Oh, I'm right. I don't think you'll find anyone who'll disagree with me. We kicked this around at the Lab for quite a spell before I came up here with it."

"Then you've undoubtedly thought of some way to get rid of them."

"Of course. That was one of the first things we did. The answer's obvious."

"Not to me."

"Sure. Starfish. They'll swamp up the extra oysters in jig time."

"But won't the starfish get too numerous?"

"No. They die off pretty fast without a source of food supply. From what we can find out about Niobe's oceans, there is virtually no acceptable food for starfish other than oysters and some microscopic animal life that wouldn't sustain an adult."

"Okay, I believe you. But you still leave me cold. I can't remember anything about a starfish that would help him break an oyster shell."

Bergdorf grinned. "I see you need a course in marine biology. Here's a thumbnail sketch. First, let's take the oyster. He has a big muscle called an adductor that closes his shell. For a while he can exert a terrific pull, but a steady tension of about nine hundred grams tires him out after an hour or so. Then the muscle relaxes and the shell gapes open. Now the starfish can exert about thirteen hundred grams of tension with his sucker-like tube feet, and since he has so many of them he doesn't have to use them all at one time. So, by shifting feet as they get tired, he can exert this pull indefinitely.

"The starfish climbs up on the oyster shell, attaches a few dozen tube feet to the outside of each valve and starts to pull. After a while the oyster gets tired, the shell opens up, and the starfish pushes its stomach out through its mouth opening, wraps the stomach around the soft parts of the oyster and digests it right in the shell!"

I shuddered.

"Gruesome, isn't it?" Bergdorf asked happily. "But it's nothing to worry about. Starfish have been eating oysters on the half shell for millions of years. In fact I'll bet that a starfish eats more oysters in its lifetime than does the most confirmed oyster-addict."

"It's not the fact that they eat them," I said feebly. "It's the way they do it. It makes me ill!"

"Why should it? After all a starfish and a human being have a lot in common. Like them, you have eaten oysters on the half shell, and they're usually alive when you gulp them down. I can't see where our digestive juices are any easier on the oyster than those of a starfish."

"Remind me never to eat another raw oyster," I said. "On second thought you won't have to. You've ruined my appetite for them forever."

Bergdorf chuckled.

"Well, now that you've disposed of one of my eating habits," I said bitterly, "let's get back to the problem. I presume that you'll have to find where the oysters are before you start in working them over with starfish."

"You've hit the reason why I'm here. That's the big problem. I want to find their source."

"Don't you know?"

"I can make a pretty good guess. You see, we picked this limb out of the Equatorial current. As you know, Varnel Island is situated right at the western termination of the current. We don't get much littoral stuff unless it comes from the Islands or West Beta. And as far as I can figure the islands are the best bet. These spat probably came from the Piralones, that island group in the middle of the current about halfway across."

I nodded. "It would be a good bet. They're uninhabited. If Harl wanted an isolated spot to conduct oyster planting experiments, I couldn't think of a better location. Nobody in his right mind would visit that place willingly. The islands support the damnedest assortment of siths you ever saw."

"If that's where it is," Bergdorf said, "we can thank heaven for the natives' suspicious nature. That location may help us save this world!"

I laughed at him. "Don't be so grim, Heinz—or so godlike. We're not going to save any worlds."

"Someone has to save them."

"We don't qualify. What we'll do is chase this business down. We'll find out where the oysters come from, get an idea of how bad things are and then let the Niobians know about it. If anyone is going to save this planet it won't be a bunch of Confederation exploration specialists."

Bergdorf sighed. "You're right, of course."

I slapped him on the shoulder. "Cheer up, Heinz." I turned to my appointment calendar and checked it over. There was nothing on it that couldn't wait a few days. "Tell you what," I continued. "I need a vacation from this place. We'll take my atomic job and go oyster hunting. It ought to be fun."

Bergdorf's grin was like a sunrise on Kardon.

*   *   *   *   *

I brought the 'copter down slowly through the overcast, feeling my way cautiously down to the ground that radar told me was somewhere below. We were hardly a hundred and fifty meters up before it became visible through the drenching tropic rain. Unless you've seen it you can't imagine what rain is really like until you've been in the Niobian tropics. It literally swamps everything, including visibility.

It was the Piralones all right.

The last time I'd seen them was when I led the rescue party that pulled Wilson Chung and his passengers out of the Baril Ocean, but they were still the same, tiny deserted spots of land surrounded by coral reefs. We were over the biggest one of the group, a rounded hummock barely a kilometer in diameter, surrounded by a barrier reef of coral. Between the reef and the island a shallow lagoon lay in sullen grayness, its surface broken into innumerable tiny wavelets by the continual splash of rain. The land itself was a solid mass of olive-green vegetation that ended abruptly at a narrow beach.

"Well, we're here," I said. "Grim looking place, isn't it?"

"Whoever spoke of the beauties of tropical islands didn't have Niobe in mind," Bergdorf agreed. "This place looks like something left behind by a cow."

I couldn't help the chuckle. The simile was too close for comfort. I tilted the rotors and we went down to hover about ten meters off the beach. Bergdorf pointed down the beach. I headed the 'copter in that direction as Bergdorf looked out of the bubble, intently scanning the waters of the lagoon. Finally he looked up with an expression of understanding on his lean face.

"No wonder I missed them!" he murmured with awe. "There are so many that there's no floor of the lagoon to spot them against. They cover the entire bottom! You might as well set her down here; it's as good a place as any."

I throttled back and landed the whirlybird on the beach. "You had your quota of vorkum?" I asked as Bergdorf reached for the door handle.

The biologist made a wry face. "Naturally. You think I'd be fool enough to go outside without it?"

"I wouldn't know. All I'm sure of is that if you're going to get out here, you'd better be loaded." I followed after him as he opened the door and jumped down to the ground.

A small horde of siths instantly left the cover of the jungle and buzzed out to investigate. A few years ago, that would have been the signal for ray beams at fan aperture, but both Bergdorf and I ignored them, trusting in the protection of the vorkum. The beasties made a tactical pass at Heinz, thought the better of it and came wheeling over in my direction. I could almost see the disappointed look in their eyes as they caught my aura, put on the brakes and returned disappointed to their shelter under the broadleaves. Whatever vorkum did, it certainly convinced insects that we were inedible and antisocial.

One or two ventured back and buzzed hopefully around our heads before giving up in disgust.

"It beats me what they live on," Bergdorf said, gesturing at the iridescent flash of the last bloodsucker as it disappeared beneath the broadleaves.

"As long as it isn't us, I don't give a damn," I said. "Maybe they live on decaying vegetable matter until something live and bloody comes along. Anyway, they seem to get along."

Bergdorf walked the few steps to the water's edge. "I won't even have to go swimming," he said as he walked into the water a few steps, bent and came up with what looked like a handful of rocks.

"Oysters?" I asked, turning one over in my hand.

"Yep. Nice little *O. lurida.* About three years old, I'd guess, and just ripe for breeding. You know, I've never seen them growing so close to the shore. They must be stacked on top of each other out there a ways. There's probably millions of them in this lagoon alone!"

"Well, we've found where they're coming from. Now all that's left is to figure out what to do about it."

"We'd still better check Beta. They might possibly have reached there."

"Not unless someone's planted them," I said. "You're forgetting the ocean currents."

"No. I was thinking of planted areas."

"Well, think again. You may know your biology, but I know Niobians. They're too suspicious to bring untried things too close to where they live. They've been that way as long as I can remember them, and I don't think that anything—even something as delightful as an oyster— would make them change overnight."

"I hope you're right."

"Oh, we'll check Beta, all right," I said. "But you can send a couple of your boys to do it. There's no sense in our wasting time with it."

I heard the noise behind us before Bergdorf did. We turned in time to see four Niobians emerge from the jungle and glide purposefully toward us. The tribal tattoos on their chests identified them as members of Tovan Harl's commune. I nudged Heinz and murmured, "We've got company."

The natives approached to within a few paces. They stood politely to leeward while one of their number approached. "I'm sorry," he said without the normal introduction, "but this is leased land. You will have to leave at once. And you will please return the oysters to the lagoon. It is not permitted to remove them."

"Oh, all right," I said. "We're through here anyway. We'll visit the other islands and then be off."

"The other islands are also leased property. When you leave I will radio the other guards, and you will not be permitted to land."

"This is not according to your customs," I protested.

"I realize that, Mr. Lanceford," the native said. "But I have given oath to keep all trespassers out."

I nodded. It wasn't usual. I wondered what Harl had in mind—possibly a planetary monopoly. If that was his plan, he was due for a surprise.

"That's very commendable," Bergdorf said, "but these oysters are going with me. They are needed as evidence."

"I'm sorry, sir," the native said. "The oysters stay here."

"Don't be a fool, Heinz," I interjected. "They're in the right. The oysters are their property. If you try to take them you'll be in trouble up to your ears."

"But I need those oysters, Arthur! Probably the only adult oyster tissue on Niobe is on these islands. I need a sample of it."

"Well, it's your neck." I turned to the native. "Don't be too hard on him," I said. "He's quite an important man."

The Niobian nodded and grinned. "Don't worry, sir. He won't feel a thing. But I really wish to apologize for our rudeness. If conditions were different—"

He paused and turned toward Bergdorf who was climbing into the 'copter with the oysters still in his hand.

*   *   *   *   *

I wasn't surprised that he didn't make it. In fact, I'd have been more surprised if he had. Heinz crumpled to the ground beside the ship. One of the natives came forward, took the oysters from his limp hand and threw them back into the lagoon.

"All right," I said to the spokesman. "You fellows clobbered him, so now you can get him into the ship."

"That is only fair," the native said. "We do not want to cause you any extra inconvenience." He gestured to his companions. Between them they got Bergdorf's limp body into the ship and strapped into one of the seats. They got out, I got in, and in a minute the two of us got out of there, going straight up through to overcast to get a celestial bearing for home.

I kept looking at Bergdorf's limp body and grinning.

It was nearly an hour later before Bergdorf woke up. "What hit me?" he asked fuzzily.

"Subsonics," I said. "They should have scared you to death."

"I fainted?"

"Sure you did. You couldn't help it. They hit like a ton of brick."

"They certainly do," he said ruefully.

"They can kill," I said. "I've seen them do it. The Niobians generate them naturally, and they can focus them fairly well. Probably this quality was one of their forms of defense against predators in their early days. It's a survival trait; and when there are enough natives present to augment the impulses they can be downright nasty."

Bergdorf nodded. "I know," he said. He stopped talking and looked out over the sun-drenched top of the overcast. "It looks like Tovan Harl wants to keep this oyster farm a private matter. In a way he's doing us a favor, but I'd still feel happier if I had one or two of those oysters."

"Why do you need them?"

"Well, I figured on getting a couple of the Navy's organic detectors and setting them for oyster protoplasm. You know how sensitive those gadgets are. There might be a small but significant change in oyster protoplasm since it has arrived here."

"Well, you don't need to worry," I said. "I put one of your pets in my pocket before the natives showed up, so you've got what you need." I pulled the oyster out and handed it to him. It didn't look any the worse for its recent rough treatment.

Bergdorf grinned. "I knew I could trust you, Chief. You're sneaky!"

I laughed at him.

*   *   *   *   *

We arrived back at Alpha without trouble. I shooed Bergdorf back to Varnel with the one oyster and a promise that I'd back him up in any requisitions he cared to make. After that I checked up on the BEE business I had neglected for the past couple of days and, finally, late that night took one of the Base's floaters and drove slowly down the trail to Kron's village.

While Earth-style civilization had done much to improve transport and communication on Niobe, it hadn't—and still hasn't for that matter—produced a highway that can stand up to the climate. Roads simply disappear in the bottomless mud. So whatever vehicular transport exists on Niobe is in the form of floaters, whose big sausage-shaped tires give enough flotation to stay on top of the ooze, and sufficient traction to move through the morass that is Niobe's surface. They're clumsy, slow and hard to steer. But they get you there—which is something you can't say about other vehicles.

Kron's village had changed somewhat since I first visited it. The industrial section was new. The serried ranks of low dural buildings gleamed metallically in the glare of the floater's lights, glistening with the sheets of water that ran from their roofs and sides. The power-broadcast station that stood in the center of the village hadn't been there either. But other than that everything was pretty much the same as it always had been, an open space in the jungle filled with stone-walled, thatch-roofed houses squatting gloomily in the endless rain.

The industry, such as it was, was concentrated solely upon the production of viscaya concentrate. It had made little difference in the Niobian way of life, which was exactly as the natives wanted it.

It was odd, I reflected, how little change had taken place in Niobian society despite better than two decades of exposure to Confederation technology. Actually, the

Confederation could leave tomorrow, and would hardly be missed. There would be no cultural vacuum. The strangers would simply be gone. Possibly some of our artifacts would be used. The atomic power-broadcast station would possibly stay, and so would the high-powered radio. Perhaps some of the gadgetry the natives had acquired from us would be used until it was worn out, but the pattern of the old ways would stay pretty much as it had always been. For Niobian culture was primarily philosophical rather than technological, and it preferred to remain that way.

I parked my floater beside the house that had sheltered Kron as long as I had known him. I entered without announcing myself.

As an old friend I had this privilege, although I seldom used it. But if I had come formally there would have been an endless rigmarole of social convention that would have had to be satisfied before we could get down to business. I didn't want to waste the time.

*   *   *   *   *

Kron was seated behind a surprisingly modern desk, reading a book by the light of a Confederation glowtube. I looked at its title—*The Analects of Confucius* and blinked. I'd heard of it. It and Machiavelli's *Prince* are classics on governmental personality and philosophy, but I had never read it. Yet here, hundreds of light years from the home world, this naked alien was reading and obviously enjoying that ancient work. It made me feel oddly ashamed of myself.

He looked up at me, nodded a greeting and laid the book down with a faint expression of regret on his doglike face. I found a chair and sat down silently. I wondered how he found time to read. My job with the BEE kept me busy every day of the 279-day year. And his, which was more important and exacting than mine, gave him time to read philosophy! I sighed. It was something I could never understand.

I waited for him to speak. As host, it was his duty to open the wall of silence which separated us.

"Greetings, friend Lanceford," Kron said. "My eyes are happy with the pleasure of beholding you." He spoke in the ancient Niobian formula of hospitality. But he made it sound as though he really meant it.

"It's a double joy to behold the face of my friend and to hear his voice," I replied in the same language. Then I switched to Confed for the business I had in mind. Their polite forms are far too clumsy and uncomfortable for business use; it takes half a day to get an idea across. "It seems as though I'm always coming to you with trouble," I began.

"What now?" Kron asked. "Every time I see you, I hope that we can relax and enjoy our friendship, but every time you are burdened. Are you Earthmen forever filled with troubles or does my world provoke them?" He smiled at me.

"A little of both, I suppose," I said.

Kron hummed—the Niobian equivalent of laughter. "I've been observing you Earthmen for the past twenty years, and I have yet to see one of you completely relaxed. You take yourselves much too seriously. After all, my friend, life is short at best. We should enjoy some of it. Now tell me your troubles, and perhaps there is no cause to worry."

"You're wrong, Kron. There is plenty of cause to worry. This can affect the well-being of everything on this world."

Kron's face sharpened into lines of interest. "Continue, friend Lanceford."

"It's those oysters the BIT sent you a few years ago. They're getting out of hand."

Kron hummed. "I was afraid that it—"

"—was something serious!" I finished. "That's what I told Heinz Bergdorf when he came to me with this story. Now sober down and listen! This *is* serious!"

*   *   *   *   *

"It sounds pretty grim," Kron said after I had finished. "But how is it that your people didn't foresee the danger? Something as viciously reproductive as the oyster should be common knowledge."

"Not on our world. You see, the study of sea life is a specialized science on Earth. It is one of the faults of our technological civilization that almost everyone must specialize from the time he enters secondary school. Unless one specializes in marine biology, one generally knows little or nothing about it."

"Odd. Very odd. But then, you Earthmen always were a peculiar race. Now, if I heard you right, I believe that you said there is an animal on your world which preys upon these oysters. A starfish?"

"Yes."

"Won't this animal be as destructive as the oyster?"

"Bergdorf doesn't think so, and I trust his judgment."

"Won't this animal also kill our Komal? They are like these oysters of yours in a way."

"But they burrow, and the starfish doesn't. They'll be safe enough."

Kron sighed. "I knew that association with you people would prove to be a mixed blessing." He shrugged his shoulders and turned his chair to his desk. A Niobian face appeared on the screen. "Call a Council meeting and let me know when it is ready," Kron ordered.

"Yes, Councilor," the face replied.

"Well, that's that. Now we can relax until the Council manages to get together."

"How long will that take?"

"I haven't the least idea," Kron said. "Several days—several weeks. It all depends upon how soon we can get enough Council members together to conduct business."

I said unhappily, "I'd like to have your outlook but we're fighting against time!"

"You Earthmen pick the most impossible opponents. You should learn to work with time rather than against it." He pulled at one ear reflectively. "You know, it is strange that your race could produce ethical philosophers like this one." He tapped the *Analects* with a webbed forefinger. "Such contrast of thought on a single world is almost incredible!"

"You haven't seen the half of it!" I chuckled. "But I'm inclined to agree with you. Earth is an incredible world."

*   *   *   *   *

Fortunately there was a battle cruiser in the Polar spaceport on a goodwill mission. We had no trouble about getting the detectors Bergdorf needed, plus a crew to run them. The Navy is co-operative about such things, and every officer knows the importance of the BEE on a planetary operation. We could have had the entire cruiser if we had wanted it.

A week later the four Marine Lab ships, each equipped with a detector, started a search of Niobe's oceans. Their atomic powerplants could drive them along at a respectable speed. Bergdorf and I expected a preliminary report within a month.

We weren't disappointed.

The results were shocking, but not unexpected. Preliminary search revealed no oysters in the other two major oceans, but the Baril Ocean was badly infested. There were groups and islands of immature oysters along the entire course of the Equatorial current and the tropical coast of Alpha. Practically every island group in the central part of the ocean showed traces of the bivalves. It was amazing how far they had spread. Even the northern shallows had a number of thriving young colonies.

Bergdorf was right. Another year and we'd have been swamped. As it was it was nothing to laugh about.

The news reached Kron just before the Council meeting, which, like most of Niobe's off-season politics, had been delayed time after time. Since a Council meeting requires an attendance of ninety per cent of the Council, it had been nearly impossible to schedule an assembly where a quorum could be present. But our news broadcasts over the BEE radio reached every corner of the planet, and the note of urgency in them finally produced results.

The Niobians held the emergency session at Base Alpha, where our radio could carry the proceedings to the entire planet. Whatever else they may be, Niobian government sessions are open to the public. Since the advent of radio, practically the entire public listens in.

Like the natives, I listened too. I wasn't surprised when Kron appeared in my office, his eyes red and swollen from lack of sleep, but with a big grin on his face that exposed his sharp sectorial teeth. "Well, that's over, friend Lanceford. Now send us your starfish."

"That's easier said than done," I replied gloomily. "I've contacted the Confederation. They won't ship twenty pounds of starfish—let alone the twenty thousand tons Bergdorf says we'll need!"

"Why not? Are they crazy? Or do they want to destroy us?"

"Neither. This is just a sample of bureaucracy at work. You see, the starfish is classed as a pest on Earth. Confederation regulations forbid the exportation of pests to member planets."

"But we need them!"

"I realize that, but the fact hasn't penetrated to the highest brass." I laughed humorlessly. "The big boys simply can't see it. By the time we marshal enough evidence to convince them, it will be too late. Knowing

how Administration operates, I'd say that it'd take at
least a year for them to become convinced. And another
two months for them to act."

"But we simply can't wait that long! Your man
Bergdorf has convinced me. We're in deadly danger!"

"You're going to have to wait," I said grimly. "Unless
you can find some way to jar them out of their rut."

Kron looked thoughtful. "I think that can be done,
friend Lanceford. As I recall, your bureaus are timid
things. Furthermore, we have something they want
pretty bad. I think we can apply pressure."

"But won't your people object? Doesn't that deny your
basic philosophy of non-interference with others?"

Kron grinned ferociously. "Not at all. Like others of
your race, you have never understood the real
significance of our social philosophy. What it actually
boils down to is simply this—we respect the customs and
desires of others but require in turn that they respect
ours."

"You mean that you will use force against the rest of
the Confederation? But you can't do that! You wouldn't
stand a chance against the Navy."

"We will first try a method we have used with our own
tribes who get out of line. I don't think anything more will
be necessary." Kron's voice was flat. "It goes against the
grain to do this, but we are left no choice." He turned and
left the room without a farewell, which was a measure of
his agitation.

I sat there behind my desk wondering what the
Niobians could do. Like my ex-boss Alvord Sims, I had a
healthy respect for them. It just could be that they could
do plenty.

They could.

*   *   *   *   *

Organization! Man, you've never seen anything like
what the Niobians tossed at our startled heads! We

always thought the Planetary Council was a loose and ineffective sort of thing, but what happened within the next twenty hours had to be seen to be believed. I saw it. But it was days before I believed it.

Within a day the natives had whipped up an organization, agreed on a plan of action and put it into effect. By noon of the next day Niobe was a closed planet. A message was sent to the Confederation informing them that Niobe was withdrawing until the emergency was over. An embargo was placed on all movement of shipping.

And everything stopped.

No factories operated. The big starfreighters stood idle and empty at the polar bases. Not one ounce of gerontin or its concentrate precursor left Niobe. Smiling groups of Niobians, using subsonics to enforce their demands, paralyzed everything the Confederation had operated on the planet. No one was hurt. The natives were still polite and friendly. But Confederation business came to an abrupt halt, and stayed halted.

It was utterly amazing! I had never heard of a planet-wide boycott before. But Niobe was entirely within her rights. The Confederation had to accept it.

And, of course, the Confederation capitulated. If the Niobians were fools enough to want pests as a condition of resuming viscaya shipments—well, it was their affair. The Confederation needed viscaya. It was willing to do almost anything to assure its continued supply.

With the full power of the Confederation turned to giving Niobe what she wanted, it wasn't long before the oysters were under control. We established a systematic seeding procedure for the starfish that kept arriving by the freighter load. In a few months Bergdorf reported that an ecological balance had been achieved.

*   *   *   *   *

"But didn't the starfish create another pest problem?" Perkins asked.

"Not at all," Lanceford said. "I told you that the Niobians had an odd sense of taste. Starfish proved to be quite acceptable to the Niobian palate. They merely added another item to Niobe's food supply."

Perkins shuddered delicately. "I wouldn't eat one of those things in a million years."

"You're going to have to eat vorkum if you expect to survive on this world. Compared to vorkum, a starfish is sheer pleasure! But that wasn't the end of it," Lanceford added with a smile. "You see, shortly after things had simmered down to normal Kron dropped into my office.

"'I think, friend Lanceford,' he said, 'that we are going to have to create a permanent organization to keep unwanted visitors out. This little affair has been a needed lesson. I have been reading about your planetary organization, and I think a thing like your Customs Service is vitally needed on our world to prevent future undesirable biological importations.'

"'I agree,' I replied. 'Anything that would prevent a repetition of this business would be advisable.'

"So that was how the Customs Service started. The insigne you will recognize as a starfish opening an oyster. Unfortunately the Niobians are quite literal minded. When they say any biological importation will be quarantined and examined, they mean Confederation citizens too!

"And that, of course, was the entering wedge. You'll find things quite homelike once you get out of here. The natives have developed an organization that's a virtual copy of our Administrative Branch. Customs, as you know, is a triumph of the bureaucratic system, and naturally the idea spread. Once the natives got used to a permanent government organization that was available at all times, it was only a question of time before the haphazard tribal organization became replaced by a planetary union. You could almost say that it was an inevitable consequence."

Lanceford grinned. "The Niobians didn't realize that the importation of foreign Customs was almost as bad as the importation of foreign animals!" He chuckled at the unconscious pun.

A Question of Courage

ILLUSTRATED BY FINLAY
ORIGINALLY PUBLISHED IN *AMAZING STORIES*
DECEMBER 1960

A Question of Courage

I smelled the trouble the moment I stepped on the lift and took the long ride up the side of the "Lachesis." There was something wrong. I couldn't put my finger on it but five years in the Navy gives a man a feeling for these things. From the outside the ship was beautiful, a gleaming shaft of duralloy, polished until she shone. Her paint and brightwork glistened. The antiradiation shields on the gun turrets and launchers were folded back exactly according to regulations. The shore uniform of the liftman was spotless and he stood at his station precisely as he should. As the lift moved slowly up past no-man's country to the life section, I noted a work party hanging precariously from a scaffolding smoothing out meteorite pits in the gleaming hull, while on the catwalk of the gantry standing beside the main cargo hatch a steady stream of supplies disappeared into the ship's belly.

I returned the crisp salutes of the white-gloved sideboys, saluted the colors, and shook hands with an immaculate ensign with an O.D. badge on his tunic.

"Glad to have you aboard, sir," the ensign said.

"I'm Marsden," I said. "Lieutenant Thomas Marsden. I have orders posting me to this ship as Executive."

"Yes, sir. We have been expecting you. I'm Ensign Halloran."

"Glad to meet you, Halloran."

"Skipper's orders, sir. You are to report to him as soon as you come aboard."

Then I got it. Everything was SOP. The ship wasn't taut, she was tight! And she wasn't happy. There was none of the devil-may-care spirit that marks crews in the Scouting Force and separates them from the stodgy mass of the Line. Every face I saw on my trip to the skipper's cabin was blank, hard-eyed, and unsmiling. There was none of the human noise that normally echoes through a

ship, no laughter, no clatter of equipment, no deviations
from the order and precision so dear to admirals' hearts.
This crew was G.I. right down to the last seam tab on
their uniforms. Whoever the skipper was, he was either
bucking for another cluster or a cold-feeling automaton to
whom the Navy Code was father, mother, and Bible.

The O.D. stopped before the closed door, executed a
mechanical right face, knocked the prescribed three times
and opened the door smartly on the heels of the word
"Come" that erupted from the inside. I stepped in
followed by the O.D.

"Commander Chase," the O.D. said. "Lieutenant
Marsden."

Chase! Not Cautious Charley Chase! I could hardly
look at the man behind the command desk. But look I
did—and my heart did a ninety degree dive straight to
the thick soles of my space boots. No wonder this ship
was sour. What else could happen with Lieutenant
Commander Charles Augustus Chase in command! He
was three classes up on me, but even though he was a
First Classman at the time I crawled out of Beast
Barracks, I knew him well. Every Midshipman in the

Academy knew him—Rule-Book Charley—By-The-Numbers Chase—his nicknames were legion and not one of them was friendly. "Lieutenant Thomas Marsden reporting for duty," I said.

He looked at the O.D. "That'll be all, Mr. Halloran," he said.

"Aye, sir," Halloran said woodenly. He stepped backward, saluted, executed a precise about face and closed the hatch softly behind him.

*   *   *   *   *

"Sit down, Marsden," Chase said. "Have a cigarette."

He didn't say, "Glad to have you aboard." But other than that he was Navy right down to the last parenthesis. His voice was the same dry schoolmaster's voice I remembered from the Academy. And his face was the same dry gray with the same fishy blue eyes and rat trap jaw. His hair was thinner, but other than that he hadn't changed. Neither the war nor the responsibilities of command appeared to have left their mark upon him. He was still the same lean, undersized square-shouldered blob of nastiness.

I took the cigarette, sat down, puffed it into a glow, and looked around the drab 6 x 8 foot cubicle called the Captain's cabin by ship designers who must have laughed as they laid out the plans. It had about the room of a good-sized coffin. A copy of the Navy Code was lying on the desk. Chase had obviously been reading his bible.

"You are three minutes late, Marsden," Chase said. "Your orders direct you to report at 0900. Do you have any explanation?"

"No, sir," I said.

"Don't let it happen again. On this ship we are prompt."

"Aye, sir," I muttered.

He smiled, a thin quirk of thin lips. "Now let me outline your duties, Marsden. You are posted to my ship as Executive Officer. An Executive Officer is the Captain's right hand."

"So I have heard," I said drily.

"Belay that, Mr. Marsden. I do not appreciate humor during duty hours."

You wouldn't, I thought.

"As I was saying, Marsden, Executive Officer, you will be responsible for—" He went on and on, covering the Code—chapter, book and verse on the duties of an Executive Officer. It made no difference that I had been Exec under Andy Royce, the skipper of the "Clotho," the ship with the biggest confirmed kill in the entire Fleet Scouting Force. I was still a new Exec, and the book said I must be briefed on my duties. So "briefed" I was—for a solid hour.

Feeling angry and tired, I finally managed to get away from Rule Book Charley and find my quarters which I shared with the Engineer. I knew him casually, a glum reservist named Allyn. I had wondered why he always seemed to have a chip on his shoulder. Now I knew.

He was lying in his shock-couch as I came in. "Welcome, sucker," he greeted me. "Glad to have you aboard."

"The feeling's not mutual," I snapped.

"What's the matter? Has the Lieutenant Commander been rolling you out on the red carpet?"

"You could call it that," I said. "I've just been told the duties of an Exec. Funny—no?"

He shook his head. "Not funny. I feel for you. He told me how to be an engineer six months ago." Allyn's thin face looked glummer than usual.

"Did I ever tell you about our skip—captain?" Allyn went on. "Or do I have to tell you? I see you're wearing an Academy ring."

"You can't tell me much I haven't already heard," I said coldly. I don't like wardroom gossips as a matter of policy. A few disgruntled men on a ship can shoot morale to hell, and on a ship this size the Exec is the morale officer. But I was torn between two desires. I wanted Allyn to go on, but I didn't want to hear what Allyn had to say. I was like the proverbial hungry mule standing halfway between two haystacks of equal size and attractiveness. And like the mule I would stand there turning my head one way and the other until I starved to death.

But Allyn solved my problem for me. "You haven't heard *this*," he said bitterly. "The whole crew applied for transfer when we came back to base after our last cruise. Of course, they didn't get it, but you get the idea. Us reservists and draftees get about the same consideration as the Admiral's dog—No! dammit!—Less than the dog. They wouldn't let a mangy cur ship out with Gutless Gus."

Gutless Gus! that was a new one. I wondered how Chase had managed to acquire that sobriquet.

* * * * *

"It was on our last patrol," Allyn went on, answering my question before I asked it. "We were out at maximum radius when the detectors showed a disturbance in normal space. Chase ordered us down from Cth for a quick look—and so help me, God, we broke out right in the middle of a Rebel supply convoy—big, fat, sitting ducks all around us. We got off about twenty Mark VII torpedoes before Chase passed the word to change over. We scooted back into Cth so fast we hardly knew we were gone. And then he raises hell with Detector section for not identifying every class of ship in that convoy!

"And when Bancroft, that's the Exec whom you've relieved, asked for a quick check to confirm our kills, Chase sat on him like a ton of brick. 'I'm not interested in how many poor devils we blew apart back there,' our Captain says. 'Our mission is to scout, to obtain information about enemy movements and get that information back to Base. We cannot transmit information from a vaporized ship, and that convoy had a naval escort. Our mission cannot be jeopardized merely to satisfy morbid curiosity. Request denied. And, Mr. Bancroft, have Communications contact Fleet. This information should be in as soon as possible.' And then he turned away leaving Bancroft biting his fingernails. He wouldn't even push out a probe—scooted right back into the blue where we'd be safe!

"You know, we haven't had one confirmed kill posted on the list since we've been in space. It's getting so we don't want to come in any more. Like the time—the 'Atropos' came in just after we touched down. She was battered—looked like she'd been through a meat grinder, but she had ten confirmed and six probable, and four of them were escorts! Hell! Our boys couldn't hold their heads up. The 'Lachesis' didn't have a mark on her and all we had was a few possible hits. You know how it goes—someone asks where you're from. You say the 'Lachesis' and they say 'Oh, yes, the cruise ship.' And that's that. It's so true you don't even feel like resenting it."

I didn't like the bitter note in Allyn's voice. He was a reservist, which made it all the worse. Reservists have ten times the outside contacts we regulars do. In general when a regular and reservist tangle, the Academy men close ranks like musk-oxen and meet the challenge with an unbroken ring of horns. But somehow I didn't feel like ringing up.

I kept hoping there was another side to the story. I'd check around and find out as soon as I got settled. And if there was another side, I was going to take Allyn apart as a malicious trouble-maker. I felt sick to my stomach.

*   *   *   *   *

We spent the next three days taking on stores and munitions, and I was too busy supervising the stowage and checking manifests to bother about running down Allyn's story. I met the other officers—Lt. Pollard the gunnery officer, Ensign Esterhazy the astrogator, and Ensign Blakiston. Nice enough guys, but all wearing that cowed, frustrated look that seemed to be a "Lachesis" trademark. Chase, meanwhile, was up in Flag Officer's Country picking up the dope on our next mission. I hoped that Allyn was wrong but the evidence all seemed to be in his favor. Even more than the officers, the crew was a mess underneath their clean uniforms. From Communications Chief CPO Haskins to Spaceman Zelinski there was about as much spirit in them as you'd find in a punishment detail polishing brightwork in Base Headquarters. I'm a cheerful soul, and usually I find no trouble getting along with a new command, but this one was different. They were efficient enough, but one could see that their hearts weren't in their work. Most crews preparing to go out are nervous and high tempered. There was none of that here. The men went through the motions with a mechanical indifference that was frightening. I had the feeling that they didn't give a damn whether they went or not—or came back or not. The indifference was so thick you could cut it with a knife. Yet there was nothing you could put your hand on. You can't touch people who don't care.

Four hours after Chase came back, we lifted gravs from Earth. Chase was sitting in the control chair, and to give him credit, we lifted as smooth as a silk scarf slipping through the fingers of a pretty woman. We hypered at eight miles and swept up through the monochromes of Cth until we hit middle blue, when Chase slipped off the helmet, unfastened his webbing, and stood up.

"Take over, Mr. Marsden," he said. "Lay a course for Parth."

"Aye, sir," I replied, slipping into the chair and fastening the web. I slipped the helmet on my head and instantly I was a part of the ship. It's a strange feeling, this synthesis of man and metal that makes a fighting ship the metallic extension of the Commander's will. I was conscious of every man on duty. What they saw I saw, what they heard I heard, through the magic of modern electronics. The only thing missing was that I couldn't feel what they felt, which perhaps was a mercy considering the condition of the crew. Using the sensor circuits in the command helmet, I let my perception roam through the ship, checking the engines, the gun crews, the navigation board, the galley—all the manifold stations of a fighting ship. Everything was secure, the ship was clean and trimmed, the generators were producing their megawatts of power without a hitch, and the converters were humming contentedly, keeping us in the blue as our speed built to fantastic levels.

I checked the course, noted it was true, set the controls on standby and relaxed, half dozing in the chair as Lume after Lume dropped astern with monotonous regularity.

An hour passed and Halloran came up to relieve me. With a sigh of relief I surrendered the chair and headset. The unconscious strain of being in rapport with ship and crew didn't hit me until I was out of the chair. But when it did, I felt like something was crushing me flat. Not that I didn't expect it, but the "Lachesis" was worse than the "Clotho" had ever been.

I had barely hit my couch when General Quarters sounded. I smothered a curse as I pounded up the companionway to my station at the bridge. Chase was there, stopwatch in hand, counting the seconds.

"Set!" Halloran barked.

"Fourteen seconds," Chase said. "Not bad. Tell the crew well done." He put the watch in his pocket and walked away.

I picked up the annunciator mike and pushed the button. "Skipper says well done," I said.

"He got ten seconds out of us once last trip," Halloran said. "And he's been trying to repeat that fluke ever since.

Bet you a munit to an 'F' ration that he'll be down with the section chief trying to shave off another second or two. Hey!—what's that—oh ..." He looked at me. "Disturbance in Cth yellow, straight down—shall we go?"

"Stop ship," I ordered. "Sound general quarters." There was no deceleration. We merely swapped ends as the alarm sounded, applied full power and stopped. That was the advantage of Cth—no inertia. We backtracked for three seconds and held in middle blue.

* * * * *

"What's going on?" Chase demanded as he came up from below. His eyes raked the instruments. "Why are we stopped?"

"Disturbance in Cth yellow, sir," I said. "We're positioned above it."

"Very good, Mr. Marsden." He took the spare helmet from the Exec's chair, clapped it on, fiddled with the controls for a moment, nodded, and took the helmet off. "Secure and resume course," he said. "That's the 'Amphitrite'—fleet supply and maintenance. One of our people."

"You sure, sir?" I asked, and then looked at the smug grin on Halloran's face and wished I hadn't asked.

"Of course," Chase said. "She's a three converter job running at full output. Since the Rebels have no three converter ships, she has to be one of ours. And since she's running at full output and only in Cth yellow, it means she's big, heavy, and awkward—which means a maintenance or an ammunition supply ship. There's an off phase beat in her number two converter that gives a twenty cycle pulse to her pattern. And the only heavy ship in the fleet with this pattern is 'Amphitrite.' You see?"

I saw—with respect. "You know all the heavies like that, sir?" I asked.

"Not all of them—but I'd like to. It's as much a part of a scoutship commander's work to know our own ships as those of the enemy."

"Could that trace be a Rebel ruse?"

"Not likely—travelling in the yellow. A ship would be cold meat this far inside our perimeter. And besides, there's no Rebel alive who can tune a converter like a Navy mechanic."

"You sure?" I persisted.

"I'm sure. But take her down if you wish."

I did. And it was the "Amphitrite."

"I served on her for six months," Chase said drily as we went back through the components. I understood his certainty now. A man has a feeling for ships if he's a good officer. But it was a trait I'd never expected in Chase. I gave the orders and we resumed our band and speed. Chase looked at me.

"You acted correctly, Mr. Marsden," he said. "Something I would hardly expect, but something I was glad to see."

"I served under Andy Royce," I reminded him.

"I know," Chase replied. "That's why I'm surprised." He turned away before I could think of an answer that would combine insolence and respect for his rank. "Keep her on course, Mr. Halloran," he tossed over his shoulder as he went out.

We kept on course—high and hard despite a couple of disturbances that lumbered by underneath us. Once I made a motion to stop ship and check, but Halloran shook his head.

"Don't do it, sir," he warned.

"Why not?"

"You heard the Captain's orders. He's a heller for having them obeyed. Besides, they might be Rebs—and we might get hurt shooting at them. We'll just report their position and approximate course—and keep on travelling. Haskins is on the Dirac right now." Halloran's voice was sarcastic.

I didn't like the sound of it, and said so.

"Well, sir—we won't lose them entirely," Halloran said comfortingly. "Some cruiser will investigate them. Chances are they're ours anyway—and if they aren't there's no sense in us risking our nice shiny skin stopping them—even though we could take them like Lundy took Koromaja. Since the book doesn't say we have to investigate, we won't." His voice was bitter again.

At 0840 hours on the fourth day out, my annunciator buzzed. "Sir," the talker's voice came over the intercom, "Lieutenants Marsden and Allyn are wanted in the Captain's quarters."

*   *   *   *   *

Chase was there—toying with the seals of a thin, brown envelope. "I have to open this in the presence of at least two officers," he said nodding at Allyn who came in behind me. "You two are senior on the ship and have the first right to know." He slid a finger through the flap.

"Effective 12, Eightmonth, GY2964," he read, "USN 'Lachesis' will proceed on offensive mission against enemy vessels as part of advance covering screen Fleet Four for major effort against enemy via sectors YD 274, YD 275, and YD 276. Entire Scouting Force IV quadrant will be grouped as Fleet Four Screen Unit under command Rear Admiral SIMMS. Initial station 'Lachesis' coordinates X 06042 Y 1327 Betelgeuse-Rigel baseline. ETA Rendezvous point 0830 plus or minus 30, 13/8/64.

"A. Evars, Fleet Admiral USN Commanding."

There it was! I could see Allyn stiffen as a peculiar sick look crossed Chase's dry face. And suddenly I heard all the ugly little nicknames—Subspace Chase, Gutless Gus, Cautious Charley—and the dozen others. For Chase was afraid. It was so obvious that not even the gray mask of his face could cover it.

Yet his voice when he spoke was the same dry, pedantic voice of old. "You have the rendezvous point, Mr.

Marsden. Have Mr. Esterhazy set the course and speed to arrive on time." He dismissed us with the traditional "That's all, gentlemen," and we went out separate ways. I didn't want to look at the triumphant smile on Allyn's face.

We hit rendezvous at 0850, picked up a message from the Admiral at 0853, and at 0855 were on our way. We were part of a broad hemispherical screen surrounding the Cruiser Force which englobed the Line and supply train—the heavies that are the backbone of any fleet. We were headed roughly in the direction of the Rebel's fourth sector, the one top-heavy with metals industries. Our exact course was known only to the brass and the computers that planned our interlock. But where we were headed wasn't important. The "Lachesis" was finally going to war! I could feel the change in the crew, the nervousness, the anticipation, the adrenal responses of fear and excitement. After a year in the doldrums, Fleet was going to try to smash the Rebels again. We hadn't done so well last time, getting ambushed in the Fifty Suns group and damn near losing our shirts before we managed to get out. The Rebs weren't as good as we were, but they were trickier, and they could fight. After all, why shouldn't they be able to? They were human, just as we were, and any one of a dozen extinct intelligent races could testify to our fighting ability, as could others not-quite-extinct. Man ruled this section of the galaxy, and someday if he didn't kill himself off in the process he'd rule all of it. He wasn't the smartest race but he was the hungriest, the fiercest, the most adaptable, and the most unrelenting. Qualities which, by the way, were exactly the ones needed to conquer a hostile universe.

But mankind was slow to learn the greatest lesson, that they *had* to cooperate if they were to go further. We were already living on borrowed time. Before the War, ten of eleven exploration ships sent into the galactic center had disappeared without a trace. Somewhere, buried deep in the billions of stars that formed the galactic hub, was a race that was as tough and tricky as we were—maybe even tougher. This was common knowledge, for the eleventh ship had returned with the news of the aliens, a story of hairbreadth escape from destruction, and a pattern of their culture which was enough like ours to frighten any thinking man. The worlds near the center of humanity's sphere realized the situation at once and quickly traded their independence for a Federal Union to pool their strength against the threat that might come any day.

But as the Union Space Navy began to take shape on the dockyards of Earth and a hundred other worlds, the independent worlds of the periphery began to eye the Union with suspicion. They had never believed the exploration report and didn't want to unite with the worlds of the center. They thought that the Union was a trick to deprive them of their fiercely cherished independence, and when the Union sent embassies to invite them into the common effort, they rejected them. And when we suggested that in the interests of racial safety they abandon their haphazard colonization efforts that resulted in an uncontrolled series of jumps into the dark, punctuated by minor wars and clashes when colonists from separate origins landed, more or less simultaneously, on a promising planet, they were certain we were up to no good.

Although we explained and showed them copies of the exploration ship's report, they were not convinced. Demagogues among them screamed about manifest destiny, independence, interference in internal affairs, and a thousand other things that made the diplomatic climate between Center and Periphery unbearably hot. And their colonists kept moving outward.

Of course the Union was not about to cooperate in this potential race suicide. We simply couldn't allow them to give that other race knowledge of our whereabouts until we were ready for them. So we informed each of the outer worlds that we would consider any further efforts at colonizing an unfriendly act, and would take steps to discourage it.

That did it.

*   *   *   *   *

We halted a few colonizing ships and sent them home under guard. We uprooted a few advance groups and returned them to their homeworlds. We established a series of observation posts to check further expansion— and six months later we were at war.

The outer worlds formed what they called a defensive league and with characteristic human rationality promptly attacked us. Naturally, they didn't get far. We had a bigger and better fleet and we were organized while they were not. And so they were utterly defeated at the Battle of Ophiuchus.

It was then that we had two choices. We could either move in and take over their defenseless worlds, or we could let them rebuild and get strong, and with their strength acquire a knowledge of cooperation—and take the chance that they would ultimately beat us. Knowing this, we wisely chose the second course and set about teaching our fellow men a lesson that was now fifteen years along and not ended yet.

By applying pressure at the right places we turned their attention inward to us rather than to the outside, and by making carefully timed sorties here and there about the periphery we forced them through sheer military necessity to gradually tighten their loosely organized League into tightly centralized authority, with the power to demand and obtain—to meet our force with counterforce. By desperate measures and straining of all their youthful resources they managed to hold us off. And with every strain they were welded more tightly together. And slowly they were learning through war what we could not teach through peace.

Curiously enough, they wouldn't believe our aims even when captured crews told them. They thought it was some sort of tricky mental conditioning designed to frustrate their lie detectors. Even while they tightened their organization and built new fleets, they would not believe that we were forcing them into the paths they must travel to avoid future annihilation.

It was one of the ironies of this war that it was fought and would be fought with the best of intentions. For it was obvious now that we could never win—nor could they. The Rebels, as we called them, were every whit as strong as we, and while we enjoyed the advantages of superior position and technology they had the advantage of superior numbers. It was stalemate,—the longest, fiercest stalemate in man's bloody history. But it was stalemate with a purpose. It was a crazy war—a period of constant hostilities mingled with sporadic offensive actions like the one we were now engaged in—but to us, at least, it was war with a purpose—the best and noblest of human purposes—the preservation of the race.

The day was coming, not too many years away, when the first of the aliens would strike the Outer worlds. Then we would unite—on the League's terms if need be—to crush the invaders and establish mankind as the supreme race in the galaxy.

But this wasn't important right now. Right now I was the Executive Officer of a scout ship commanded by a man I didn't trust. He smelled too much like a stinking coward. I shook my head. Having Chase running the ship was like putting a moron in a jet car on one of the superhighways—and then sabotaging the automatics. Just one fearful mistake and a whole squadron could be loused up. But Chase was the commander—the ultimate authority on this ship. All I could do was pray that things were going to come out all right.

We moved out in the lower red. Battles weren't fought in Cth. There was no way to locate a unit at firing range in that monochromatic madness. Normal physical laws simply didn't apply. A ship had to come out into threespace to do any damage. All Cth was was a convenient road to the battlefront.

With one exception.

By hanging in the infra band, on the ragged edge of threespace, a scout ship could remain concealed until a critical moment, breakout into threespace—discharge her weapons—and flick back into Cth before an enemy could get a fix on her. Scouts, with their high capacity converters, could perform this maneuver, but the ponderous battlewagons and cruisers with their tremendous weight of armor, screens, and munitions couldn't maneuver like this. They simply didn't have the agility. Yet only they had the ability to penetrate defensive screens and kill the Rebel heavies. So space battle was conducted on the classic pattern—the Lines slugging it out at medium range while the screen of scouts buzzed around and through the battle trying to add their weight of metal against some overstrained enemy and ensure his destruction. A major battle could go on for days—and it often did. In the Fifty Suns action the battle had lasted nearly two weeks subjective before we withdrew to lick our wounds.

*   *   *   *   *

For nearly a day we ran into nothing, and such are the distances that separate units of a fleet, we had the impression that we were alone. We moved quietly, detectors out, scanning the area for a light-day around as we moved forward at less than one Lume through Cth. More would have been fatal for had we been forced to resort to a quick breakout to avoid enemy action, and if we were travelling above one Lume when we hit threespace, we'd simply disappear, leaving a small spatial vortex in our wake.

On the "morning" of the third day the ships at the apex of Quadrant One ran into a flight of Rebel scouts.

There was a brief flurry of action, the Rebels were englobed, a couple of cruisers drove in, latched onto the helplessly straining Rebel scouts and dragged them into threespace. The Rebs kept broadcasting right up to the end—after which they surrendered before the cruisers could annihilate them. Smart boys.

But the Rebels were warned. We couldn't catch all their scouts and the disturbance our Line was making in Cth would register on any detector within twenty parsecs. So they would be waiting to meet us. But that was to be expected. There is no such thing as surprise in a major action.

We went on until we began to run into major opposition. Half a dozen scouts were caught in englobements at half a dozen different places along the periphery as they came in contact with the Rebels' covering forces. And that was that. The advance halted waiting for the Line to come up, and a host of small actions took place as the forward screening forces collided. Chase was in the control chair, hanging in the blackness of the infra band on the edge of normal space. But we weren't flicking in and out of threespace like some of the others. We had a probe out and the main buffeting was taken by the duralloy tube with its tiny converter at its bulbous tip. With consummate pilotage Chase was holding us in infra. It was a queasy sensation, hanging halfway between normalcy and chaos, and I had to admire his skill. The infra band was black as ink and hot as the hinges of hell—and since the edges of threespace and Cth are not as knife sharp as they are further up in the Cth components, we bucked and shuddered on the border, but avoided the bone-crushing slams and gut-wrenching twists that less skillful skippers were giving their ships as they flicked back and forth between threespace and Cth. Our scouting line must have been a peculiar sight to a threespace observer with the thousand or so scouts flickering in and out of sight across a huge hemisphere of space.

And then we saw them. Our probe picked up the flicker of enemy scouts.

"Action imminent," Chase said drily. "Stand by."

I clapped the other control helmet over my head and dropped into the Exec's chair. A quick check showed the crew at their stations, the torpedo hatches clear, the antiradiation shields up and the ship in fighting trim. I stole a quick glance at Chase. Sweat stood out on his gray forehead. His lips were drawn back into a thin line, showing his teeth. His face was tense, but whether with fear or excitement I didn't know.

"Stand by," he said, and then we hit threespace, just as the enormous cone of the Rebel Line flicked into sight. The enemy line had taken the field, and under the comparatively slow speeds of threespace was rushing forward to meet our Line which had emerged a few minutes ago. Our launchers flamed as we sent a salvo of torpedoes whistling toward the Rebel fleet marking perhaps the opening shots of the main battle. We twisted back into Cth as one of the scanner men doubled over with agony, heaving his guts out into a disposal cone. I felt sorry for him. The tension, the racking agony of our motion, and the fact that he was probably in his first major battle had all combined to take him for the count. He grinned greenly at me and turned back to his dials and instruments. Good man!

"Target—range one eight zero four, azimuth two four oh, elevation one oh seven," the rangefinder reported. "Mass four." Mass four:—a cruiser.

"Stand by," Chase said. "All turrets prepare to fire." And he took us down. We slammed into threespace and our turrets flamed. To our left rear and above hung the mass of an enemy cruiser, her screens glowing on standby as she drove forward to her place in the line. We had caught her by surprise, a thousand to one shot, and our torpedoes were on their way before her detectors spotted us. We didn't stay to see what happened, but the probe showed an enormous fireball which blazed briefly in the blackness, shooting out globs of scintillating molten metal that cooled and disappeared as we watched.

"Scratch one cruiser," someone in fire control yelped.

*   *   *   *   *

The effect on morale was electric. In that instant all doubts of Chase's ability disappeared. All except mine. One lucky shot isn't a battle, and I guess Chase figured the same way because his hands were shaking as he jockeyed us along on the edge of Cth. He looked like he wanted to vomit.

"Take it easy, skipper," I said.

"Mind your own business, Marsden—and I'll mind mine," Chase snapped. "Stand by," he ordered, and we dove into threespace again—loosed another salvo at another Reb, and flicked out of sight. And that was the way it went for hour after hour until we pulled out, our last torpedo fired and the crew on the ragged edge of exhaustion. Somehow, by some miracle compounded of luck and good pilotage, we were unmarked. And Chase, despite his twitching face and shaking hands, was one hell of a combat skipper! I didn't wonder about him any more. He had the guts all right. But it was a different sort of courage from the icy contempt for danger that marked Andy Royce. Even so, I couldn't help thinking that I was glad to be riding with Chase. We drove to the rear, heading for the supply train, our ammunition expended, while behind us the battlewagons and cruisers were hammering each other to metal pulp.

In the quiet of the rear area it was hardly believable that a major battle was going on ahead of us. We raised the "Amphitrite," identified ourselves, and put in a request for supply.

"Lay aboard," "Amphitrite" signalled back. "How's the war going?"

"Don't know. We've been too busy," our signalman replied.

"I'll bet—you're 'Lachesis,' aren't you?"

"Affirmative."

"How'd you lose your ammo? Jettison it?"

"Stow that, you unprintable obscenity," Haskins replied. "We're a fighting ship."

"Amphitrite" chuckled nastily. "That I'll believe when I see it!"

"Communications," Chase snapped. "This isn't a social call. Get our heading and approach instructions." He sounded as schoolmasterish as ever, but there was a sickly smile on his face, and the gray-green look was gone.

"Morale seems a little better, doesn't it, Marsden?" he said to me as the "Amphitrite" flicked out into threespace and we followed.

I nodded. "Yes, sir," I agreed. "Quite a little."

Our cargo hatches snapped open and we cuddled up against "Amphitrite's" bulging belly while our crew and the supply echelon worked like demons to transfer ammunition. We had fifty torpedoes aboard when the I.F.F. detector shrilled alarm.

Three hundred feet above us the "Amphitrite's" main battery let loose a salvo at three Rebel scouts that had flickered into being less than fifty miles away. Their launchers flared with a glow that lighted the blackness of space.

"Stand by!" Chase yelled as he threw the converter on.

"Hatches!" I screamed as we shimmered and vanished.

Somehow we got most of them closed, losing only the crew on number two port turret which was still buttoning up as we slipped over into the infra band. I ordered the turret sealed. Cth had already ruined the unshielded sighting mechanisms and I had already seen what happened to men caught in Cth unprotected. I had no desire to see it again—or let our crew see it if it could be avoided. A human body turned inside out isn't the most wholesome of sights.

"How did *they* get through?" Chase muttered as we put out our probe.

"I don't know—maybe someone wasn't looking."

"What's it like down there?" Chase asked. "See anything?"

"'Amphitrite's' still there," I said.

"She's *what?*"

"Still there," I repeated. "And she's in trouble."

"She's big. She can take it—but—"

"Here, you look," I said, flipping the probe switch.

"My God!" Chase muttered—as he took one look at the supply ship lying dead in space, her protective batteries flaming. She had gotten one of the Rebel scouts but the other two had her bracketed and were pouring fire against her dim screens.

"She can't keep this up," I said. "She's been hulled—and it looks like her power's taken it."

"Action imminent," Chase ordered, and the rangefinder took up his chant.

We came storming out of Cth right on top of one of the Rebel scouts. A violent shock raced through the ship, slamming me against my web. The rebound sent us a good two miles away before our starboard battery flamed. The enemy scout, disabled by the shock, stunned and unable to maneuver took the entire salvo amidships and disappeared in a puff of flame.

The second Rebel disappeared and we did too. She was back in Cth looking for a better chance at the "Amphitrite." The big ship was wallowing like a wounded whale, half of one section torn away, her armor dented, and her tubes firing erratically.

We took one long look and jumped back into Cth. But not before Haskins beamed a message to the supply ship. "Now you've seen it, you damned storekeeper," he gloated. "What do you think?" "Amphitrite" didn't answer.

"Probe out," Chase ordered, neglecting, I noticed, to comment on the signalman's act.

*   *   *   *   *

I pushed the proper buttons but nothing happened. I pushed again and then turned on the scanners. The one aft of the probe was half covered with a twisted mass of metal tubing that had once been our probe. We must have smashed it when we rammed. Quickly I shifted to the auxiliary probe, but the crumpled mass had jammed the hatch. It wouldn't open.

"No probes, sir," I announced.

"Damn," Chase said. "Well, we'll have to do without them. Hold tight, we're going down."

We flicked into threespace just in time to see a volcano of fire erupt from "Amphitrite's" side and the metallic flick of the Rebel scout slipping back into Cth.

"What's your situation, 'Amphitrite'?" our signal asked.

"Not good," the faint answer came back. "They've got us in the power room and our accumulators aren't going to stand this load very long. That last salvo went through our screens, but our armor stopped it. But if the screens go down—"

Our batteries flared at the Rebel as he again came into sight. He didn't wait, but flicked right back into Cth without firing a shot. Pollard was on the ball.

"Brave lad, that Reb," Chase said. There was a sneer in his voice.

For the moment it was stalemate. The Reb wasn't going to come into close range with a warship of equal power to his own adding her metal to the "Amphitrite's," but he could play cat and mouse with us, drawing our fire until we had used up our torpedoes, and then come in to finish the supply ship. Or he could harass us with long range fire. Or he could go away.

It was certain he wouldn't do the last, and he'd be a fool if he did the second. "Amphitrite" could set up a mine screen that would take care of any long range stuff,—and we could dodge it. His probe was still working and he had undoubtedly seen ours crushed against our hull. If he hadn't he was blind—and that wasn't a Rebel characteristic. We could hyper, of course, but we were blind up there in Cth. His best was to keep needling us, and take the chance that we'd run out of torps.

"What's our munition?" Chase asked almost as an echo to my thought. I switched over to Pollard.

"Thirty mark sevens," Pollard said, "and a little small arms."

"One good salvo," Chase said, thoughtfully.

The Rebel flashed in and out again, and we let go a burst.

"Twenty, now," I said.

Chase didn't hear me. He was busy talking to Allyn on damage control. "You can't cut it, hey?—All right—disengage the converter on the auxiliary probe and break out that roll of duralloy cable in the stores—Pollard! don't fire over one torp at a time when that lad shows up. Load the other launchers with blanks. Make him think we're shooting. We have to keep him hopping. Now listen to me—Yes, Allyn, I mean you. Fasten that converter onto the cable and stand by. We're going to make a probe." Chase turned to me.

"You were Exec with Royce," he said. "You should know how to fight a ship."

"What are you planning to do?" I asked.

"We can't hold that Rebel off. Maybe with ammunition we could, but there's less than a salvo aboard and he has the advantage of position. We can't be sure he won't try to take us in spite of 'Amphitrite's' support and if he does finish us, 'Amphitrite's' a dead duck." The "Lachesis" quivered as the port turrets belched flame. "That leaves nineteen torpedoes," he said. "In Cth we're safe enough but we're helpless without a probe. Yet we can only get into attack position from Cth. That leaves us only one thing to do—improvise a probe."

"And how do you do that?" I asked.

"Put a man out on a line—with the converter from the auxiliary. Give him a command helmet and have him talk the ship in."

"But that's suicide!"

"No, Marsden, not suicide—just something necessary. A necessary sacrifice, like this whole damned war! I don't believe in killing men. It makes me sick. But I kill if I have to, and sacrifice if I must." His face twisted and the gray-green look came back. "There are over a thousand men on the 'Amphitrite,' and a vital cargo of munitions. One life, I think, is fair trade for a thousand, just as a few hundred thousand is fair trade for a race." The words were schoolmasterish and would have been dead wrong coming from anyone except Chase. But he gave them an air of reasonable inevitability. And for a moment I forgot that he was cold-bloodedly planning someone's death. For a moment I felt the spirit of sacrifice that made heroes out of ordinary people.

*   *   *   *   *

"Look, skipper," I said. "How about letting me do it?" I could have kicked myself a moment later, but the words were out before I could stop them. He had me acting noble, and that trait isn't one of my strong suits.

He smiled. "You know, Marsden," he said, "I was expecting that." His voice was oddly soft. "Thanks." Then it became dry and impersonal. "Request denied," he said. "This is my party."

I shivered inside. While I'm no coward, I didn't relish the thought of slamming around at the end of a duralloy cable stretching into a nowhere where there was no inertia. A hair too heavy a hand on the throttle in Cth would crush the man on the end to a pulp. But he shouldn't go either. It was his responsibility to command the ship.

"Who else is qualified?" Chase said answering the look on my face. "I know more about maneuver than any man aboard, and I'll be controlling the ship until the last moment. Once I order the attack I'll cut free, and you can pick me up later."

"You won't have time," I protested.

"Just in case I don't make it," Chase continued, making the understatement of the war with a perfectly straight face, "take care of the crew. They're a good bunch—just a bit too eager for the *real* Navy—but good. I've tried to make them into spacemen and they've resented me for it. I've tried to protect them and they've hated me—"

"They won't now—" I interrupted.

"I've tried to make them a unit." He went on as though I hadn't said a thing. "Maybe I've tried too hard, but I'm responsible for every life aboard this ship." He picked up his helmet. "Take command of the ship, Mr. Marsden," he said, and strode out of the room. The "Lachesis" shuddered to the recoil from the port turrets. Eighteen torpedoes left, I thought.

We lowered Chase a full hundred feet on the thin strand of duralloy. He dangled under the ship, using his converter to keep the line taut.

"You hear me, skipper?" I asked.

"Clearly—and you?"

"Four-four. Hang on now—we're going up." I eased the "Lachesis" into Cth and hung like glue to the border. "How's it going, skipper?"

"A bit rough but otherwise all right. Now steer right—easy now—aagh!"

"Skipper!"

"Okay, Marsden. You nearly pulled me in half—that's all. You did fine. We're in good position in relation to 'Amphitrite.' Now let's get our signals straight. Front is the way we're going now—base all my directions on that—got it?"

"Aye, sir."

"Good, Marsden, throttle back and hang on your converters."

I did as I was told.

"Ah—there she is—bear left a little. Hmm—she's looking for us—looks suspicious. Now she's turning toward 'Amphitrite.' Guess she figures we are gone. She's in position preparing to fire. *Now!* Drop out and fire—elevation zero, azimuth three sixty—*Move!*"

I moved. The "Lachesis" dropped like a stone. Chase was dead now. Nothing made of flesh could survive that punishment but we—we came out right on top of them, just like Chase had done to the other—except that we fired before we collided. And as with the other Rebel we gained complete surprise. Our eighteen torpedoes crashed home, her magazines exploded, and into that hell of molten and vaporized metal that had once been a Rebel scout we crashed a split second later. Two thousand miles per second relative is too fast for even an explosion to hurt much if there isn't any solid material in the way, but even so, the vaporized metal scoured our starboard plating down to the insulation. It was like a giant emery wheel had passed across our flank. The shock slammed us out of control and we went tumbling in crazy gyrations across space for several minutes before I could flip the

"Lachesis" into Cth, check the speed and motion, and get back into threespace.

*   *   *   *   *

Chase was gone—and "Lachesis" was done. A week in drydock and she'd be as good as new, but she was no longer a fighting ship. She was a wreck. For us the battle was over—but somehow it didn't make me happy. The "Amphitrite" hung off our port bow, a tiny silver dot in the distance, and as I watched two more silver dots winked into being beside her. Haskins reported the I.F.F. readings.

"They're ours," he said. "A couple of cruisers."

"They should have been here ten minutes ago," I replied bitterly. I couldn't see very well. You can't when emotion clogs your tubes. Chase—coward?—not him. He was man clear through—a better one than I'd ever be even if I lived out my two hundred years. I wondered if the crew knew what sort of man their skipper was. I turned up the command helmet. "Men—" I began, but I didn't finish.

"We know," the blended thoughts and voices came back at me. Sure they knew! Chase had been on command circuit too. It was enough to make you cry—the mixture of pride, sadness and shame that rang through the helmet. It seemed to echo and reecho for a long time before I shut it off.

I sat there, thinking. I wasn't mad at the Rebels. I wasn't anything. All I could think was that we were paying a pretty grim price for survival. Those aliens had better show up pretty soon and they'd better be as nasty as their reputation. There was a score—a big score—and I wanted to be there when it was added up and settled.

A Prize for Edie

Illustrated by Schoenherr
Originally Published In
Analog Science Fact
and Science Fiction
April 1961

*The Committee had,
unquestionably, made a
mistake. There was no doubt
that Edie had achieved the
long-sought cancer cure ...
but awarding the Nobel
Prize was, nonetheless, a
mistake...*

A Prize for Edie

The letter from America arrived too late. The Committee had regarded acceptance as a foregone conclusion, for no one since Boris Pasternak had turned down a Nobel Prize. So when Professor Doctor Nels Christianson opened the letter, there was not the slightest fear on his part, or on that of his fellow committeemen, Dr. Eric Carlstrom and Dr. Sven Eklund, that the letter would be anything other than the usual routine acceptance.

"At last we learn the identity of this great research worker," Christianson murmured as he scanned the closely typed sheets. Carlstrom and Eklund waited impatiently, wondering at the peculiar expression that fixed itself on Christianson's face. Fine beads of sweat appeared on the professor's high narrow forehead as he laid the letter down. "Well," he said heavily, "now we know."

"Know what?" Eklund demanded. "What does it say? Does she accept?"

"She accepts," Christianson said in a peculiar half-strangled tone as he passed the letter to Eklund. "See for yourself."

Eklund's reaction was different. His face was a mottled reddish white as he finished the letter and handed it across the table to Carlstrom. "Why," he demanded of no one in particular, "did this have to happen to us?"

"It was bound to happen sometime," Carlstrom said. "It's just our misfortune that it happened to us." He chuckled as he passed the letter back to Christianson. "At least this year the presentation should be an event worth remembering."

"It seems that we have a little problem," Christianson said, making what would probably be the understatement of the century. Possibly there would be greater understatements in the remaining ninety-nine years of the Twenty-first Century, but Carlstrom doubted it. "We certainly have our necks out," he agreed.

"We can't do it!" Eklund exploded. "We simply can't award the Nobel Prize in medicine and physiology to that ... that *C. Edie!*" He sputtered into silence.

"We can hardly do anything else," Christianson said. "There's no question as to the identity of the winner. Dr. Hanson's letter makes that unmistakably clear. And there's no question that the award is deserved."

"We still could award it to someone else," Eklund said.

"Not a chance. We've already said too much to the press. It's known all over the world that the medical award is going to the discoverer of the basic cause of cancer, to the founder of modern neoplastic therapy." Christianson grimaced. "If we changed our decision now, there'd be all sorts of embarrassing questions from the press."

"I can see it now," Carlstrom said, "the banquet, the table, the flowers, and Professor Doctor Nels Christianson in formal dress with the Order of St. Olaf gleaming across his white shirtfront, standing before that distinguished audience and announcing: 'The Nobel Prize in Medicine and Physiology is awarded to—' and then that deadly hush when the audience sees the winner."

"You needn't rub it in," Christianson said unhappily. "I can see it, too."

"These Americans!" Eklund said bitterly. He wiped his damp forehead. The picture Carlstrom had drawn was accurate but hardly appealing. "One simply can't trust them. Publishing a report as important as that as a laboratory release. They should have given proper credit."

"They did," Carlstrom said. "They did—precisely. But the world, including us, was too stupid to see it. We have only ourselves to blame."

"If it weren't for the fact that the work was inspired and effective," Christianson muttered, "we might have a chance of salvaging this situation. But through its application ninety-five per cent of cancers are now curable. It is obviously the outstanding contribution to medicine in the past five decades."

"But we must consider the source," Eklund protested. "This award will make the prize for medicine a laughingstock. No doctor will ever accept another. If we go through with this, we might as well forget about the medical award from now on. This will be its swan song. It hits too close to home. Too many people have been saying similar things about our profession and its trend toward specialization. And to have the Nobel Prize confirm them would alienate every doctor in the world. We simply can't do it."

"Yet who else has made a comparable discovery? Or one that is even half as important?" Christianson asked.

"That's a good question," Carlstrom said, "and a good answer to it isn't going to be easy to find. For my part, I can only wish that Alphax Laboratories had displayed an interest in literature rather than medicine. Then our colleagues at the Academy could have had the painful decision."

"Their task would be easier than ours," Christianson said wearily. "After all, the criteria of art are more flexible. Medicine, unfortunately, is based upon facts."

"That's the hell of it," Carlstrom said.

"There must be some way to solve this problem," Eklund said. "After all it was a perfectly natural mistake. We never suspected that Alphax was a physical rather than a biological sciences laboratory. Perhaps that might offer grounds—"

"I don't think so," Carlstrom interrupted. "The means in this case aren't as important as the results, and we can't deny that the cancer problem is virtually solved."

"Even though men have been saying for the past two generations that the answer was probably in the literature and all that was needed was someone with the intelligence and the time to put the facts together, the fact remains that it was C. Edie who did the job. And it required quite a bit more than merely collecting facts. Intelligence and original thinking of a high order was involved." Christianson sighed.

"Some*one*," Eklund said bitterly. "Some *thing* you mean. *C. Edie*—C.E.D.—Computer, Extrapolating, Discriminatory. Manufactured by Alphax Laboratories, Trenton, New Jersey, U.S.A. *C. Edie!* Americans!!— always naming things. A machine wins the Nobel Prize. It's fantastic!"

Christianson shook his head. "It's not fantastic, unfortunately. And I see no way out. We can't even award the prize to the team of engineers who designed and built Edie. Dr. Hanson is right when he says the discovery was Edie's and not the engineers'. It would be like giving the prize to Albert Einstein's parents because they created him."

*   *   *   *   *

"Is there any way we can keep the presentation secret?" Eklund asked.

"I'm afraid not. The presentations are public. We've done too good a job publicizing the Nobel Prize. As a telecast item, it's almost the equal of the motion picture Academy Award."

"I can imagine the reaction when our candidate is revealed in all her metallic glory. A two-meter cube of steel filled with microminiaturized circuits, complete with flashing lights and cogwheels," Carlstrom chuckled. "And where are you going to hang the medal?"

Christianson shivered. "I wish you wouldn't give that metal nightmare a personality," he said. "It unnerves me. Personally, I wish that Dr. Hanson, Alphax Laboratories, and Edie were all at the bottom of the ocean—in some nice deep spot like the Mariannas Trench." He shrugged. "Of course, we won't have that sort of luck, so we'll have to make the best of it."

"It just goes to show that you can't trust Americans," Eklund said. "I've always thought we should keep our awards on this side of the Atlantic where people are sane and civilized. Making a personality out of a computer—ugh! I suppose it's their idea of a joke."

"I doubt it," Christianson said. "They just like to name things—preferably with female names. It's a form of insecurity, the mother fixation. But that's not important. I'm afraid, gentlemen, that we shall have to make the award as we have planned. I can see no way out. After all, there's no reason why the machine cannot receive the prize. The conditions merely state that it is to be presented to the one, regardless of nationality, who makes the greatest contribution to medicine or physiology."

"I wonder how His Majesty will take it," Carlstrom said.

"The king! I'd forgotten that!" Eklund gasped.

"I expect he'll have to take it," Christianson said. "He might even appreciate the humor in the situation."

"Gustaf Adolf is a good king, but there are limits," Eklund observed.

"There are other considerations," Christianson replied. "After all, Edie is the reason the Crown Prince is still alive, and Gustaf is fond of his son."

"After all these years?"

Christianson smiled. Swedish royalty *was* long-lived. It was something of a standing joke that King Gustaf would probably outlast the pyramids, providing the pyramids lived in Sweden. "I'm sure His Majesty will cooperate. He has a strong sense of duty and since the real problem is his, not ours, I doubt if he will shirk it."

"How do you figure that?" Eklund asked.

"We merely select the candidates according to the rules, and according to the nature of their contribution. Edie is obviously the outstanding candidate in medicine for this year. It deserves the prize. We would be compromising with principle if we did not award it fairly."

"I suppose you're right," Eklund said gloomily. "I can't think of any reasonable excuse to deny the award."

"Nor I," Carlstrom said. "But what did you mean by that remark about this being the king's problem?"

"You forget," Christianson said mildly. "Of all of us, the king has the most difficult part. As you know, the Nobel Prize is formally presented at a State banquet."

"Well?"

"His Majesty is the host," Christianson said. "And just how does one eat dinner with an electronic computer?"

PANDEMIC

ILLUSTRATED BY BARBERIS
ORIGINALLY PUBLISHED IN *ANALOG SCIENCE FACT
AND SCIENCE FICTION*
FEBRUARY 1962

PANDEMIC

Generally, human beings don't do totally useless things consistently and widely. So—maybe there is something to it—

"We call it Thurston's Disease for two perfectly good reasons," Dr. Walter Kramer said. "He discovered it—and he was the first to die of it." The doctor fumbled fruitlessly through the pockets of his lab coat. "Now where the devil did I put those matches?"

"Are these what you're looking for?" the trim blonde in the gray seersucker uniform asked. She picked a small box of wooden safety matches from the littered lab table beside her and handed them to him.

"Ah," Kramer said. "Thanks. Things have a habit of getting lost around here."

"I can believe that," she said as she eyed the frenzied disorder around her. Her boss wasn't much better than his laboratory, she decided as she watched him strike a match against the side of the box and apply the flame to the charred bowl of his pipe. His long dark face became half obscured behind a cloud of bluish smoke as he puffed furiously. He looked like a lean untidy devil recently escaped from hell with his thick brows, green eyes and lank black hair highlighted intermittently by the leaping flame of the match. He certainly didn't look like a pathologist. She wondered if she was going to like working with him, and shook her head imperceptibly. Possibly, but not probably. It might be difficult being cooped up here with him day after day. Well, she could always quit if things got too tough. At least there was that consolation.

He draped his lean body across a lab stool and leaned his elbows on its back. There was a faint smile on his face as he eyed her quizzically. "You're new," he said. "Not just to this lab but to the Institute."

She nodded. "I am, but how did you know?"

"Thurston's Disease. Everyone in the Institute knows that name for the plague, but few outsiders do." He smiled sardonically. "Virus pneumonic plague—that's a better term for public use. After all, what good does it do to advertise a doctor's stupidity?"

She eyed him curiously. "*De mortuis?*" she asked.

He nodded. "That's about it. We may condemn our own, but we don't like laymen doing it. And besides, Thurston had good intentions. He never dreamed this would happen."

"The road to hell, so I hear, is paved with good intentions."

"Undoubtedly," Kramer said dryly. "Incidentally, did you apply for this job or were you assigned?"

"I applied."

"Someone should have warned you I dislike cliches," he said. He paused a moment and eyed her curiously. "Just why did you apply?" he asked. "Why are you imprisoning yourself in a sealed laboratory which you won't leave as long as you work here. You know, of course, what the conditions are. Unless you resign or are carried out feet first you will remain here ... have you considered what such an imprisonment means?"

"I considered it," she said, "and it doesn't make any difference. I have no ties outside and I thought I could help. I've had training. I was a nurse before I was married."

"Divorced?"

"Widowed."

Kramer nodded. There were plenty of widows and widowers outside. Too many. But it wasn't much worse than in the Institute where, despite precautions, Thurston's disease took its toll of life.

"Did they tell you this place is called the suicide section?" he asked.

She nodded.

"Weren't you frightened?"

"Of dying? Hardly. Too many people are doing it nowadays."

He grimaced, looking more satanic than ever. "You have a point," he admitted, "but it isn't a good one. Young people should be afraid of dying."

"You're not."

"I'm not young. I'm thirty-five, and besides, this is my business. I've been looking at death for eleven years. I'm immune."

"I haven't your experience," she admitted, "but I have your attitude."

"What's your name?" Kramer said.

"Barton, Mary Barton."

"Hm-m-m. Well, Mary—I can't turn you down. I need you. But I could wish you had taken some other job."

"I'll survive."

He looked at her with faint admiration in his greenish eyes. "Perhaps you will," he said. "All right. As to your duties—you will be my assistant, which means you'll be a dishwasher, laboratory technician, secretary, junior pathologist, and coffee maker. I'll help you with all the jobs except the last one. I make lousy coffee." Kramer grinned, his teeth a white flash across the darkness of his face. "You'll be on call twenty-four hours a day, underpaid, overworked, and in constant danger until we lick Thurston's virus. You'll be expected to handle the jobs of three people unless I can get more help—and I doubt that I can. People stay away from here in droves. There's no future in it."

Mary smiled wryly. "Literally or figuratively?" she asked.

He chuckled. "You have a nice sense of graveyard humor," he said. "It'll help. But don't get careless. Assistants are hard to find."

She shook her head. "I won't. While I'm not afraid of dying I don't want to do it. And I have no illusions about the danger. I was briefed quite thoroughly."

"They wanted you to work upstairs?"

She nodded.

*   *   *   *   *

"I suppose they need help, too. Thurston's Disease has riddled the medical profession. Just don't forget that this place can be a death trap. One mistake and you've had it. Naturally, we take every precaution, but with a virus no protection is absolute. If you're careless and make errors in procedure, sooner or later one of those submicroscopic protein molecules will get into your system."

"You're still alive."

"So I am," Kramer said, "but I don't take chances. My predecessor, my secretary, my lab technician, my junior pathologist, and my dishwasher all died of Thurston's Disease." He eyed her grimly. "Still want the job?" he asked.

"I lost a husband and a three-year old son," Mary said with equal grimness. "That's why I'm here. I want to destroy the thing that killed my family. I want to do something. I want to be useful."

He nodded. "I think you can be," he said quietly.

"Mind if I smoke?" she asked. "I need some defense against that pipe of yours."

"No—go ahead. Out here it's all right, but not in the security section."

Mary took a package of cigarettes from her pocket, lit one and blew a cloud of gray smoke to mingle with the blue haze from Kramer's pipe.

"Comfortable?" Kramer asked.

She nodded.

He looked at his wrist watch. "We have half an hour before the roll tube cultures are ready for examination. That should be enough to tell you about the modern

Pasteur and his mutant virus. Since your duties will primarily involve Thurston's Disease, you'd better know something about it." He settled himself more comfortably across the lab bench and went on talking in a dry schoolmasterish voice. "Alan Thurston was an immunologist at Midwestern University Medical School. Like most men in the teaching trade, he also had a research project. If it worked out, he'd be one of the great names in medicine; like Jenner, Pasteur, and Salk. The result was that he pushed it and wasn't too careful. He wanted to be famous."

"He's well known now," Mary said, "at least within the profession."

"Quite," Kramer said dryly. "He was working with gamma radiations on microorganisms, trying to produce a mutated strain of *Micrococcus pyogenes* that would have enhanced antigenic properties."

"Wait a minute, doctor. It's been four years since I was active in nursing. Translation, please."

Kramer chuckled. "He was trying to make a vaccine out of a common infectious organism. You may know it better as *Staphylococcus*. As you know, it's a pus former that's made hospital life more dangerous than it should be because it develops resistance to antibiotics. What Thurston wanted to do was to produce a strain that would stimulate resistance in the patient without causing disease—something that would help patients protect themselves rather than rely upon doubtfully effective antibiotics."

"That wasn't a bad idea."

"There was nothing wrong with it. The only trouble was that he wound up with something else entirely. He was like the man who wanted to make a plastic suitable for children's toys and ended up with a new explosive. You see, what Thurston didn't realize was that his cultures were contaminated. He'd secured them from the University Clinic and had, so he thought, isolated them.

But somehow he'd brought a virus along—probably one of the orphan group or possibly a phage."

"Orphan?"

"Yes—one that was not a normal inhabitant of human tissues. At any rate there was a virus—and he mutated it rather than the bacteria. Actually, it was simple enough, relatively speaking, since a virus is infinitely simpler in structure than a bacterium, and hence much easier to modify with ionizing radiation. So he didn't produce an antigen—he produced a disease instead. Naturally, he contracted it, and during the period between his infection and death he managed to infect the entire hospital. Before anyone realized what they were dealing with, the disease jumped from the hospital to the college, and from the college to the city, and from the city to—"

"Yes, I know that part of it. It's all over the world now—killing people by the millions."

*   *   *   *   *

"Well," Kramer said, "at least it's solved the population explosion." He blew a cloud of blue smoke in Mary's direction. "And it did make Thurston famous. His name won't be quickly forgotten."

She coughed. "I doubt if it ever will be," she said, "but it won't be remembered the way he intended."

He looked at her suspiciously. "That cough—"

"No, it's not Thurston's Disease. It's that pipe. It's rancid."

"It helps me think," Kramer said.

"You could try cigarettes—or candy," she suggested.

"I'd rather smoke a pipe."

"There's cancer of the lip and tongue," she said helpfully.

"Don't quote Ochsner. I don't agree with him. And besides, you smoke cigarettes, which are infinitely worse."

"Only four or five a day. I don't saturate my system with nicotine."

"In another generation," Kramer observed, "you'd have run through the streets of the city brandishing an ax smashing saloons. You're a lineal descendent of Carrie Nation." He puffed quietly until his head was surrounded by a nimbus of smoke. "Stop trying to reform me," he added. "You haven't been here long enough."

"Not even God could do that, according to the reports I've heard," she said.

He laughed. "I suppose my reputation gets around."

"It does. You're an opinionated slave driver, a bully, an intellectual tyrant, and the best pathologist in this center."

"The last part of that sentence makes up for unflattering honesty of the first," Kramer said. "At any rate, once we realized the situation we went to work to correct it. Institutes like this were established everywhere the disease appeared for the sole purpose of examining, treating, and experimenting with the hope of finding a cure. This section exists for the evaluation of treatment. We check the human cases, and the primates in the experimental laboratories. It is our duty to find out if anything the boys upstairs try shows any promise. We were a pretty big section once, but Thurston's virus has whittled us down. Right now there is just you and me. But there's still enough work to keep us busy. The experiments are still going on, and there are still human cases, even though the virus has killed off most of the susceptibles. We've evaluated over a thousand different drugs and treatments in this Institute alone."

"And none of them have worked?"

"No—but that doesn't mean the work's been useless. The research has saved others thousands of man hours chasing false leads. In this business negative results are almost as important as positive ones. We may never discover the solution, but our work will keep others from making the same mistakes."

"I never thought of it that way."

"People seldom do. But if you realize that this is international, that every worker on Thurston's Disease has a niche to fill, the picture will be clearer. We're doing our part inside the plan. Others are, too. And there are thousands of labs involved. Somewhere, someone will find the answer. It probably won't be us, but we'll help get the problem solved as quickly as possible. That's the important thing. It's the biggest challenge the race has ever faced—and the most important. It's a question of survival." Kramer's voice was sober. "We have to solve this. If Thurston's Disease isn't checked, the human race will become extinct. As a result, for the first time in history all mankind is working together."

"All? You mean the Communists are, too?"

"Of course. What's an ideology if there are no people to follow it?" Kramer knocked the ashes out of his pipe, looked at the laboratory clock and shrugged. "Ten minutes more," he said, "and these tubes will be ready. Keep an eye on that clock and let me know. Meantime you can straighten up this lab and find out where things are. I'll be in the office checking the progress reports." He turned abruptly away, leaving her standing in the middle of the cluttered laboratory.

"Now what am I supposed to do here?" Mary wondered aloud. "Clean up, he says. Find out where things are, he says. Get acquainted with the place, he says. I could spend a month doing that." She looked at the littered bench, the wall cabinets with sliding doors half open, the jars of reagents sitting on the sink, the drainboard, on top of the refrigerator and on the floor. The disorder was appalling. "How he ever manages to work in here is beyond me. I suppose that I'd better start somewhere—perhaps I can get these bottles in some sort of order first." She sighed and moved toward the wall cabinets. "Oh well," she mused, "I asked for this."

*   *   *   *   *

"Didn't you hear that buzzer?" Kramer asked.

"Was that for me?" Mary said, looking up from a pile of bottles and glassware she was sorting.

"Partly. It means they've sent us another post-mortem from upstairs."

"What is it?"

"I don't know—man or monkey, it makes no difference. Whatever it is, it's Thurston's Disease. Come along. You might as well see what goes on in our ultra modern necropsy suite."

"I'd like to." She put down the bottle she was holding and followed him to a green door at the rear of the laboratory.

"Inside," Kramer said, "you will find a small anteroom, a shower, and a dressing room. Strip, shower, and put on a clean set of lab coveralls and slippers which you will find in the dressing room. You'll find surgical masks in the wall cabinet beside the lockers. Go through the door beyond the dressing room and wait for me there. I'll give you ten minutes."

*   *   *   *   *

"We do this both ways," Kramer said as he joined her in the narrow hall beyond the dressing room. "We'll reverse the process going out."

"You certainly carry security to a maximum," she said through the mask that covered the lower part of her face.

"You haven't seen anything yet," he said as he opened a door in the hall. "Note the positive air pressure," he said. "Theoretically nothing can get in here except what we bring with us. And we try not to bring anything." He stood aside to show her the glassed-in cubicle overhanging a bare room dominated by a polished steel post-mortem table that glittered in the harsh fluorescent lighting. Above the table a number of jointed rods and clamps hung from the ceiling. A low metal door and series

of racks containing instruments and glassware were set
into the opposite wall together with the gaping circular
orifice of an open autoclave.

"We work by remote control, just like they do at the
AEC. See those handlers?" He pointed to the control
console set into a small stainless steel table standing
beside the sheet of glass at the far end of the cubicle.
"They're connected to those gadgets up there." He
indicated the jointed arms hanging over the autopsy table
in the room beyond. "I could perform a major operation
from here and never touch the patient. Using these I can
do anything I could in person with the difference that
there's a quarter inch of glass between me and my work. I
have controls that let me use magnifiers, and even do
microdissection, if necessary."

"Where's the cadaver?" Mary asked.

"Across the room, behind that door," he said, waving
at the low, sliding metal partition behind the table. "It's
been prepped, decontaminated and ready to go."

"What happens when you're through?"

"Watch." Dr. Kramer pressed a button on the console
in front of him. A section of flooring slid aside and the
table tipped. "The cadaver slides off that table and
through that hole. Down below is a highly efficient
crematorium."

Mary shivered. "Neat and effective," she said shakily.

"After that the whole room is sprayed with germicide
and sterilized with live steam. The instruments go into
the autoclave, and thirty minutes later we're ready for
another post-mortem."

"We use the handlers to put specimens into those
jars," he said, pointing to a row of capped glass jars of
assorted sizes on a wall rack behind the table. "After
they're capped, the jars go onto that carrier beside the
table. From here they pass through a decontamination
chamber and into the remote-control laboratory across
the hall where we can run biochemical and histological
techniques. Finished slides and mounted specimens then

go through another decontamination process to the outside lab. Theoretically, this place is proof against anything."

"It seems to be," Mary said, obviously impressed. "I've never seen anything so elegant."

"Neither did I until Thurston's Disease became a problem." Kramer shrugged and sat down behind the controls. "Watch, now," he said as he pressed a button. "Let's see what's on deck—man or monkey. Want to make a bet? I'll give you two to one it's a monkey."

She shook her head.

* * * * *

The low door slid aside and a steel carriage emerged into the necropsy room bearing the nude body of a man. The corpse gleamed pallidly under the harsh shadowless glare of the fluorescents in the ceiling as Kramer, using the handlers, rolled it onto the post-mortem table and clamped it in place on its back. He pushed another button and the carriage moved back into the wall and the steel door slid shut. "That'll be decontaminated," he said, "and sent back upstairs for another body. I'd have lost," he remarked idly. "Lately the posts have been running three to one in favor of monkeys."

He moved a handler and picked up a heavy scalpel from the instrument rack. "There's a certain advantage to this," he said as he moved the handler delicately. "These gadgets give a tremendous mechanical advantage. I can cut right through small bones and cartilage without using a saw."

"How nice," Mary said. "I expect you enjoy yourself."

"I couldn't ask for better equipment," he replied noncommittally. With deft motion of the handler he drew the scalpel down across the chest and along the costal margins in the classic inverted "Y" incision. "We'll take a look at the thorax first," he said, as he used the handlers to pry open the rib cage and expose the thoracic viscera. "Ah! Thought so! See that?" He pointed with a small handler that carried a probe. "Look at those lungs." He swung a viewer into place so Mary could see better. "Look at those abscesses and necrosis. It's Thurston's Disease, all right, with secondary bacterial invasion."

The grayish solidified masses of tissue looked nothing like the normal pink appearance of healthy lungs. Studded with yellowish spherical abscesses they lay swollen and engorged within the gaping cavity of the chest.

"You know the pathogenesis of Thurston's Disease?" Kramer asked.

Mary shook her head, her face yellowish-white in the glare of the fluorescents.

"It begins with a bronchial cough," Kramer said. "The virus attacks the bronchioles first, destroys them, and passes into the deeper tissues of the lungs. As with most virus diseases there is a transitory leukopenia—a drop in the total number of white blood cells—and a rise in temperature of about two or three degrees. As the virus attacks the alveolar structures, the temperature rises and the white blood cell count becomes elevated. The lungs become inflamed and painful. There is a considerable quantity of lymphoid exudate and pleural effusion. Secondary invaders and pus-forming bacteria follow the viral destruction of the lung tissue and form abscesses. Breathing becomes progressively more difficult as more lung tissue is destroyed. Hepatization and necrosis inactivate more lung tissue as the bacteria get in their dirty work, and finally the patient suffocates."

"But what if the bacteria are controlled by antibiotics?"

"Then the virus does the job. It produces atelectasis followed by progressive necrosis of lung tissue with gradual liquefaction of the parenchyma. It's slower, but just as fatal. This fellow was lucky. He apparently stayed out of here until he was almost dead. Probably he's had the disease for about a week. If he'd have come in early, we could have kept him alive for maybe a month. The end, however, would have been the same."

"It's a terrible thing," Mary said faintly.

"You'll get used to it. We get one or two every day." He shrugged. "There's nothing here that's interesting," he said as he released the clamps and tilted the table. For what seemed to Mary an interminable time, the cadaver clung to the polished steel. Then abruptly it slid off the shining surface and disappeared through the square hole in the floor. "We'll clean up now," Kramer said as he placed the instruments in the autoclave, closed the door and locked it, and pressed three buttons on the console.

From jets embedded in the walls a fine spray filled the room with fog.

"Germicide," Kramer said. "Later there'll be steam. That's all for now. Do you want to go?"

Mary nodded.

"If you feel a little rocky there's a bottle of Scotch in my desk. I'll split a drink with you when we get out of here."

"Thanks," Mary said. "I think I could use one."

*   *   *   *   *

"Barton! Where is the MacNeal stain!" Kramer's voice came from the lab. "I left it on the sink and it's gone!"

"It's with the other blood stains and reagents. Second drawer from the right in the big cabinet. There's a label on the drawer," Mary called from the office. "If you can wait until I finish filing these papers, I'll come in and help you."

"I wish you would," Kramer's voice was faintly exasperated. "Ever since you've organized my lab I can't find anything."

"You just have a disorderly mind," Mary said, as she slipped the last paper into its proper folder and closed the file. "I'll be with you in a minute."

"I don't dare lose you," Kramer said as Mary came into the lab. "You've made yourself indispensable. It'd take me six months to undo what you've done in one. Not that I mind," he amended, "but I was used to things the way they were." He looked around the orderly laboratory with a mixture of pride and annoyance. "Things are so neat they're almost painful."

"You look more like a pathologist should," Mary said as she deftly removed the tray of blood slides from in front of him and began to run the stains. "It's my job to keep you free to think."

"Whose brilliant idea is that? Yours?"

"No—the Director's. He told me what my duties were when I came here. And I think he's right. You should be using your brain rather than fooling around with blood stains and sectioning tissues."

"But I like to do things like that," Kramer protested. "It's relaxing."

"What right have you to relax," Mary said. "Outside, people are dying by the thousands and you want to relax. Have you looked at the latest mortality reports?"

"No—"

"You should. The WHO estimates that nearly two billion people have died since Thurston's Disease first appeared in epidemic proportions. That's two out of three. And more are dying every day. Yet you want to relax."

"I know," Kramer said, "but what can we do about it. We're working but we're getting no results."

"You might use that brain of yours," Mary said bitterly. "You're supposed to be a scientist. You have facts. Can't you put them together?"

"I don't know." He shrugged, "I've been working on this problem longer than you think. I come down here at night—"

"I know. I clean up after you."

"I haven't gotten anywhere. Sure, we can isolate the virus. It grows nicely on monkey lung cells. But that doesn't help. The thing has no apparent antigenicity. It parasitizes, but it doesn't trigger any immune reaction. We can kill it, but the strength of the germicide is too great for living tissue to tolerate."

"Some people seem to be immune."

"Sure they do—but why?"

"Don't ask me. I'm not the scientist."

"Play like one," Kramer growled. "Here are the facts. The disease attacks people of all races and ages. So far every one who is attacked dies. Adult Europeans and Americans appear to be somewhat more resistant than others on a population basis. Somewhere around sixty per cent of them are still alive, but it's wiped out better than eighty per cent of some groups. Children get it worse. Right now I doubt if one per cent of the children born during the past ten years are still alive."

"It's awful!" Mary said.

"It's worse than that. It's extinction. Without kids the race will die out." Kramer rubbed his forehead.

"Have you any ideas?"

"Children have less resistance," Kramer replied. "An adult gets exposed to a number of diseases to which he builds an immunity. Possibly one of these has a cross immunity against Thurston's virus."

"Then why don't you work on that line?" Mary asked.

"Just what do you think I've been doing? That idea was put out months ago, and everyone has been taking a crack at it. There are twenty-four laboratories working full time on that facet and God knows how many more working part time like we are. I've screened a dozen common diseases, including the six varieties of the common cold virus. All, incidentally, were negative."

"Well—are you going to keep on with it?"

"I have to." Kramer rubbed his eyes. "It won't let me sleep. I'm sure we're on the right track. Something an adult gets gives him resistance or immunity." He shrugged. "Tell you what. You run those bloods out and I'll go take another look at the data." He reached into his lab coat and produced a pipe. "I'll give it another try."

"Sometimes I wish you'd read without puffing on that thing," Mary said.

"Your delicate nose will be the death of me yet—" Kramer said.

"It's my lungs I'm worried about," Mary said. "They'll probably look like two pieces of well-tanned leather if I associate with you for another year."

"Stop complaining. You've gotten me to wear clean lab coats. Be satisfied with a limited victory," Kramer said absently, his eyes staring unseeingly at a row of reagent bottles on the bench. Abruptly he nodded. "Fantastic," he muttered, "but it's worth a check." He left the room, slamming the door behind him in his hurry.

*   *   *   *   *

"That man!" Mary murmured. "He'd drive a saint out of his mind. If I wasn't so fond of him I'd quit. If anyone told me I'd fall in love with a pathologist, I'd have said they were crazy. I wish—" Whatever the wish was, it wasn't uttered. Mary gasped and coughed rackingly.

Carefully she moved back from the bench, opened a drawer and found a thermometer. She put it in her mouth. Then she drew a drop of blood from her forefinger and filled a red and white cell pipette, and made a smear of the remainder.

She was interrupted by another spasm of coughing, but she waited until the paroxysm passed and went methodically back to her self-appointed task. She had done this many times before. It was routine procedure to check on anything that might be Thurston's Disease. A cold, a sore throat, a slight difficulty in breathing—all demanded the diagnostic check. It was as much a habit as breathing. This was probably the result of that cold she'd gotten last week, but there was nothing like being sure. Now let's see—temperature 99.5 degrees, red cell count 4-1/2 million. White cell count ... oh! 2500 ... leukopenia! The differential showed a virtual absence of polymorphs, lymphocytes and monocytes. The whole slide didn't have two hundred. Eosinophils and basophils way up—twenty and fifteen per cent respectively—a relative rise rather than an absolute one—leukopenia, no doubt about it.

She shrugged. There wasn't much question. She had Thurston's Disease. It was the beginning stages, the harsh cough, the slight temperature, the leukopenia. Pretty soon her white cell count would begin to rise, but it would rise too late. In fact, it was already too late. It's funny, she thought. I'm going to die, but it doesn't frighten me. In fact, the only thing that bothers me is that poor Walter is going to have a terrible time finding things. But I can't put this place the way it was. I couldn't hope to.

She shook her head, slid gingerly off the lab stool and went to the hall door. She'd better check in at the clinic, she thought. There was bed space in the hospital now. Plenty of it. That hadn't been true a few months ago but the only ones who were dying now were the newborn and an occasional adult like herself. The epidemic had died out not because of lack of virulence but because of lack of victims. The city outside, one of the first affected, now had less than forty per cent of its people left alive. It was a hollow shell of its former self. People walked its streets and went through the motions of life. But they were not really alive. The vital criteria were as necessary for a race as for an individual. Growth, reproduction, irritability, metabolism—Mary smiled wryly. Whoever had authored that hackneyed mnemonic that life was a "grim" proposition never knew how right he was, particularly when one of the criteria was missing.

The race couldn't reproduce. That was the true horror of Thurston's Disease—not how it killed, but who it killed. No children played in the parks and playgrounds. The schools were empty. No babies were pushed in carriages or taken on tours through the supermarkets in shopping carts. No advertisements of motherhood, or children, or children's things were in the newspapers or magazines. They were forbidden subjects—too dangerously emotional to touch. Laughter and shrill young voices had vanished from the earth to be replaced by the drab grayness of silence and waiting. Death had laid cold hands upon the hearts of mankind and the survivors were frozen to numbness.

*   *   *   *   *

It was odd, she thought, how wrong the prophets were. When Thurston's Disease broke into the news there were frightened predictions of the end of civilization. But they had not materialized. There were no mass insurrections, no rioting, no organized violence. Individual excesses, yes—but nothing of a group nature. What little panic there was at the beginning disappeared once people realized that there was no place to go. And a grim passivity had settled upon the survivors. Civilization did not break down. It endured. The mechanics remained intact. People had to do something even if it was only routine counterfeit of normal life—the stiff upper lip in the face of disaster.

It would have been far more odd, Mary decided, if mankind had given way to panic. Humanity had survived other plagues nearly as terrible as this—and racial memory is long. The same grim patience of the past was here in the present. Man would somehow survive, and civilization go on.

It was inconceivable that mankind would become extinct. The whole vast resources and pooled intelligence of surviving humanity were focused upon Thurston's Disease. And the disease would yield. Humanity waited with childlike confidence for the miracle that would save it. And the miracle would happen, Mary knew it with a calm certainty as she stood in the cross corridor at the end of the hall, looking down the thirty yards of tile that separated her from the elevator that would carry her up to the clinic and oblivion. It might be too late for her, but not for the race. Nature had tried unaided to destroy man before—and had failed. And her unholy alliance with man's genius would also fail.

She wondered as she walked down the corridor if the others who had sickened and died felt as she did. She speculated with grim amusement whether Walter Kramer would be as impersonal as he was with the others, when he performed the post-mortem on her body. She shivered at the thought of that bare sterile room and the shining table. Death was not a pretty thing. But she could meet it with resignation if not with courage. She had already seen too much for it to have any meaning. She did not falter as she placed a finger on the elevator button.

Poor Walter—she sighed. Sometimes it was harder to be among the living. It was good that she didn't let him know how she felt. She had sensed a change in him recently. His friendly impersonality had become merely friendly. It could, with a little encouragement, have developed into something else. But it wouldn't now. She sighed again. His hardness had been a tower of strength. And his bitter gallows humor had furnished a wry relief to grim reality. It had been nice to work with him. She wondered if he would miss her. Her lips curled in a faint smile. He would, if only for the trouble he would have in making chaos out of the order she had created. Why couldn't that elevator hurry?

*   *   *   *   *

"Mary! Where are you going?" Kramer's voice was in her ears, and his hand was on her shoulder.

"Don't touch me!"

"Why not?" His voice was curiously different. Younger, excited.

"I have Thurston's Disease," she said.

He didn't let go. "Are you sure?"

"The presumptive tests were positive."

"Initial stages?"

She nodded. "I had the first coughing attack a few minutes ago."

He pulled her away from the elevator door that suddenly slid open. "You were going to that death trap upstairs," he said.

"Where else can I go?"

"With me," he said. "I think I can help you."

"How? Have you found a cure for the virus?"

"I think so. At least it's a better possibility than the things they're using up there." His voice was urgent. "And to think I might never have seen it if you hadn't put me on the track."

"Are you sure you're right?"

"Not absolutely, but the facts fit. The theory's good."

"Then I'm going to the clinic. I can't risk infecting you. I'm a carrier now. I can kill you, and you're too important to die."

"You don't know how wrong you are," Kramer said.

"Let go of me!"

"No—you're coming back!"

She twisted in his grasp. "Let me go!" she sobbed and broke into a fit of coughing worse than before.

"What I was trying to say," Dr. Kramer said into the silence that followed, "is that if you have Thurston's Disease, you've been a carrier for at least two weeks. If I am going to get it, your going away can't help. And if I'm not, I'm not."

"Do you come willingly or shall I knock you unconscious and drag you back?" Kramer asked.

She looked at his face. It was grimmer than she had ever seen it before. Numbly she let him lead her back to the laboratory.

*   *   *   *   *

"But, Walter—I can't. That's sixty in the past ten hours!" she protested.

"Take it," he said grimly, "then take another. And inhale. Deeply."

"But they make me dizzy."

"Better dizzy than dead. And, by the way—how's your chest?"

"Better. There's no pain now. But the cough is worse."

"It should be."

"Why?"

"You've never smoked enough to get a cigarette cough," he said.

She shook her head dizzily. "You're so right," she said.

"And that's what nearly killed you," he finished triumphantly.

"Are you sure?"

"I'm certain. Naturally, I can't prove it—yet. But that's just a matter of time. Your response just about clinches it. Take a look at the records. Who gets this disease? Youngsters—with nearly one hundred per cent morbidity and one hundred per cent mortality. Adults— less than fifty per cent morbidity—and again one hundred per cent mortality. What makes the other fifty per cent immune? Your crack about leather lungs started me thinking—so I fed the data cards into the computer and keyed them for smoking versus incidence. And I found that not one heavy smoker had died of Thurston's Disease. Light smokers and nonsmokers—plenty of them—but not one single nicotine addict. And there were over ten thousand randomized cards in that spot check. And there's the exact reverse of that classic experiment the lung cancer boys used to sell their case. Among certain religious groups which prohibit smoking there was nearly one hundred per cent mortality of all ages!

"And so I thought since the disease was just starting in you, perhaps I could stop it if I loaded you with tobacco smoke. And it works!"

"You're not certain yet," Mary said. "I might not have had the disease."

"You had the symptoms. And there's virus in your sputum."

"Yes, but—"

"But, nothing! I've passed the word—and the boys in the other labs figure that there's merit in it. We're going to call it Barton's Therapy in your honor. It's going to cause a minor social revolution. A lot of laws are going to have to be rewritten. I can see where it's going to be illegal for children not to smoke. Funny, isn't it?

"I've contacted the maternity ward. They have three babies still alive upstairs. We get all the newborn in this town, or didn't you know. Funny, isn't it, how we still try to reproduce. They're rigging a smoke chamber for the kids. The head nurse is screaming like a wounded tiger, but she'll feel better with live babies to care for. The only bad thing I can see is that it may cut down on her chain smoking. She's been worried a lot about infant mortality.

"And speaking of nurseries—that reminds me. I wanted to ask you something."

"Yes?"

"Will you marry me? I've wanted to ask you before, but I didn't dare. Now I think you owe me something— your life. And I'd like to take care of it from now on."

"Of course I will," Mary said. "And I have reasons, too. If I marry you, you can't possibly do that silly thing you plan."

"What thing?"

"Naming the treatment Barton's. It'll have to be Kramer's."

And Now a Message . . .
By Greg Fowlkes

A short Story from the upcoming Book - *Back Road to the Stars*

And Now A Message...

For the third time that night Jack Olsen was about to nod off over the copy of *Statistical Information Theory* that he was attempting to read. Giving it up as a bad effort, he shut the book and looked out the window of the control room at the giant bowl of the Arecibo radio telescope. Theoretically he was running the huge instrument, but in reality all the controlling was being done by the computers in the room around him. For six months he had been working eight hour shifts every night, and his job had consisted of the five minutes a shift that it took to enter the coordinates to be examined on the control console. Other than that, he was on hand only for the off chance that the monitoring programs would recognize some pattern in the radio noise, in which case an alarm would sound. So far, in the six months, it hadn't happened.

He walked over to the coffee machine in the hopes that a cup would revive him enough so that he could continue his studies. He never made it, for as if to prove the lie of his earlier thoughts, the alarm sounded. For a moment Jack was frozen, the alarm beating raucously in his ears, then he pulled himself together and flicked off the switch on the bell. With the room returned to the relative quiet of the whoosh of the cooling fans on the equipment, Jack sat down at the console and keyed in an enquiry. Within seconds the computer had replied that it was receiving a strong periodic signal on the 42 centimeter band. Further questioning showed that it was not a program malfunction but a genuine signal.

Jack picked up the phone and dialed his boss's number. It was three in the morning, but his instructions had been clear. If anything was received that could possibly be an intelligent signal, he was supposed to contact his superior immediately.

Despite the long drive through the mountains in the cool Puerto Rican night, Professor Kraft showed up with his eyes still sleepy. Shuffling over to the coffee pot by the window he poured himself a large mug before he said anything. "You'd better have something good to get me up at this hour."

"I think so," Jack said, aware that his boss's irritation was only feigned. "I've been checking with the computer since I called you. It shows a strong periodic signal with a sharp pulse every fifty milliseconds. It runs on like that for about two and a half minutes before the signal fades below the background."

"Any chance that it might be a pulsar?" Kraft asked, referring to the radio signals of rapidly rotating neutron stars. "That's within the range of periods for them. When the first one was discovered, they thought that they had received intelligent signals."

"I thought of that, so I checked the record of the broad band receiver." Jack brought out a long strip of graph paper and pointed to the evenly spaced patterns of peaks on it. "Where the narrow band shows only a single repetitive pulse, the wide band gives us this fine structure. It's far too regular to be a pulsar and much too detailed. It's more like some sort of timing signal or spacer. And in between the pulses there is another signal. It's not as repetitive as the main pulse. That's why the program doesn't bring it out. But there definitely is some sort of transmission in between. It's weaker, but I think that we can write a processing program to pick it out from the noise."

Kraft looked at the trace in his hand thoughtfully. "I hate to make snap judgements. You can be suckered in too easily that way. But it does look like some kind of artificial signal. We'll get the team working on it in the morning. Have you received any additional signals?"

"No. I've kept the dish tracking the source, but all we get on 42 cm. is background noise. It's like there was a moment of freak atmospheric conditions that opened a window, and then it shut again. Just like you get with shortwave sometimes because of the ionosphere."

"Well, we should be grateful for what we've got. I don't think I can sleep anymore tonight, so I'll keep you company. I'd like to be here if we get any more messages from our friends out there," he said, pointing with his cup towards the star filled sky that loomed over the radio telescope's antenna.

"Frustrating, isn't it?" Prof. Kraft remarked to the team of graduate students and post doctoral fellows that were working under him on the interstellar communications project. And frustrating it had been. For six months they had continuously monitored the sky searching for signs of life finally to be rewarded by a two minute snippet of extraterrestrial conversation.

Now, another six months later, they had still made no sense of the signal, nor had they received any further transmissions from that part of the sky, though they had concentrated their efforts in that direction.

"Rumors have leaked out about our discovery, and I've been getting requests for the data. I'd sure hate to have someone else steal our thunder by deciphering the signal, but if we don't make some progress soon, we're going to have to release it." He looked around the table at the young faces of his assistants. At the moment they didn't look nearly as bright and intelligent as he knew they were.

"Why don't I summarize what we've found so far in hopes that it will give us some new ideas?"

"First, we've got this repetitive pattern of pulses every twentieth of a second as regular as clockwork. So regular, in fact, that we can't decide whether they serve as breaks in the message or were just put there to attract our attention. Remember, it was these pulses that were first recognized by the computer."

"But the pulses aren't the real message. That lays in the spaces in between. We've been able to deduce that the messages are digitized and the computer has been able to enhance them so that we have a fairly error free record of them. There is some repetitive structure to them, and they do vary in some sort of progression, but beyond that, we haven't been able to get the least notion of what they mean. Anyone have something to add?"

Bill Warden, one of the post docs, spoke up. "Well, we've tried mathematical analysis on the signals and have gotten zero results. It has already been assumed that any sort of interstellar communications would be based on sort of easily recognizable mathematical progression. Like one, two three. Something like that to show that they were rational. From there you can always build up more complicated concepts."

"With this message we don't have that, which leads us to one of two assumptions. One, we have only a fragment of a broadcast, and from a very advanced lesson at that. If that's the case, I don't see much hope of our being able to decipher the message until we can receive more signals to give us a broader base to work from."

"The other alternative is that they, whoever they are, just don't think like us. Their minds work in some fashion so that this mess we have makes sense to them. If so, I don't see any hope at all. Their minds may just be too foreign for us to hold a dialog with them."

"Thank you for that optimistic note," Prof. Kraft said wryly. "For the first time mankind has received a message from another species and we can't tell whether it is a cure for cancer, a means of achieving universal peace, or a recipe for sauerbratten. Any comments?"

"If it's sauerbratten, where do we go for a tablespoon of powdered bandersnatch egg?" quipped one of the grad students. They all laughed at the joke more than it deserved. Six months of unrewarded work had left them all a little giddy. After the giggles and comments had died down, Jack Olsen coughed, trying to get their attention.

"You've got something useful to say, Jack?" Kraft asked. "You might as well tell us. I don't think anyone else has anything useful to add," he said, pointedly looking at the wisecracker.

"I've been thinking about the signal, and I remember something that I said to you the night it came in. I don't know if you recall, but I called the pulses timing signals. Now there is one type of common transmission that has the same kind of pulses, and that's television. They use the pulses to synchronize the frames. It's possible that the message in between each pulse is a picture, and the whole transmission is meant to be viewed in sequence."

"How long have you been sitting on this while the rest of us were beating our brains out?" Kraft asked.

"It just came to me," Jack said, his face flushed. "I should have thought of it earlier, but like Bill said, we've all been conditioned to look for something like one plus one equals two."

"I think that we should all have seen it," Kraft said. "It makes as much sense as anything else that's been suggested. Do you think that you can get us a picture?"

"If it's there, I should be able to pick it out using the computer," Jack answered.

"Good. Then, since it was your idea, you're in charge. Dragoon anything or anybody that you need to help you."

Five days later they were all gathered around the conference room table again, but this time there was a TV set and a video recorder on a cart at its end. From the nervous stubbing of cigarette butts and fingers drumming on the table, it was obvious that all the members of the team were in a state of anticipation.

"It took some time to figure out exactly how the signal was put together," Jack began. "After all, we didn't know how many lines there were in each frame or how many bits made up each unit of picture. In the end, I had to have the computer run through all the likely possibilities for one of the frames. It took a lot of computer time, but I've finally got some recognizable pictures."

"It turns out that the original broadcast was in color. That threw us for a while, but we finally psyched it out. The aliens must have eyes structurally different from ours; there are only two colors, not three in the signal. Which colors they are is anybody's guess. They might be ultraviolet and infrared for all we can tell. Arbitrarily, I've assigned them red and bluish green, so keep that in mind. Also, because the video recorder uses thirty frames a second instead of the twenty in the transmission, it was necessary to compress the program a bit. This means that everything you'll be seeing has been speeded up about fifty percent.

"I guess you're all more interested in seeing the tape than in listening to me." A snort from Prof. Kraft indicated agreement. Jack flicked off the lights and started the tape. For a minute the screen showed only snow, then a face became recognizable. It was a sickly chartreuse, and there was no nose between the two large, oval eyes, but it was recognizable as a face. The figures movements were quick and jerky like an old silent movie, the result of the difference in frame speed, and the picture left a lot to be desired in clarity, the product of interstellar noise, but it was a picture, the first of an alien race.

As the tape played, a weird, sings song voice came from the speaker sounding something like a Chinese chipmunk. "I forgot to mention that there was also an audio track along with the signal. Again, it's only a reconstruction and may not bear much resemblance to the original, but then, we'll never know," Jack commented. They had determined that the source of the transmission was at least several dozen light years away. It would take twice that number of years to send a message and receive a reply, by which time they would all be dead.

They continued to watch the tape. The camera had drawn back to show the alien from the waist up revealing rounded shoulders and a pair of six fingered hands. Apparently he was standing behind a low lectern or a table of some sort. The fuzzy picture and camera angle made it hard to tell which. As he, or her, or it, spoke, the alien pointed at a chart or poster suspended on the backdrop. A pattern of red and blue that hurt the eye with violent contrasts seemed to be some sort of text. The voice continued as the picture disappeared in a sea of snow and then it broke into static. The transmission had ended.

"You've done a fine job, Jack," Prof. Kraft said after they had played the tape through a half dozen times. "It's actually far better than I thought it would be, and I think we can accept any of the shortcomings that you mentioned."

"So, we've got a face and body of what certainly is a rational creature. He seemed to be giving us a lesson or lecture of some sort, though I for one don't have the faintest idea of what he was talking about. We have an idea of what they look like which I am sure will give the biologists a lot to speculate on, so I guess that we should be thankful for small favors, but I still don't see how we're going to learn any more about them without receiving further signals."

"I wouldn't hold out much hope of that," Jack interjected. "I think that it's clear now that the signal we picked up was not meant for interstellar communication. Any such signal would have been designed with much greater noise immunity. We were able to receive it only because of an accident of atmospheric conditions. It was actually just a local TV broadcast. As we haven't received anything since, those conditions must be rare."

"So," Kraft said, "we have a message of great potential import, that at the very least could provide us with insights on a totally alien culture, and no way to decipher it."

"I've got an idea," Bill said. "We've all been looking at the problem from the point of view of hardware and computer programs. That's natural because of our backgrounds, but now that we have what amounts to an artifact, maybe we should call in a specialist. We need someone who is trained in resurrecting a culture from its fragments. I suggest that we show the tape to some archeologists and get their opinions."

Convincing an archeologist to look at the tape was harder than it had sounded. Most of them were more interested in ancient rather than alien civilizations. Jack suspected that they felt out of their depth with the computers and electronics. With some pressure and pleading, a group finally agreed to view the tape, but after the showing, only one evinced any interest in following up on it.

A visiting lecturer from Norway, she was reputed to have a good background in languages, though Jack lacked the knowledge to judge her qualifications. However, as she was young, blond, and attractive, he was quite willing to spend the time required to familiarize her with the tape and the equipment they had used to come up with it. Together, they spent hours viewing the tape, studying it frame by frame attempting to pick out the slightest piece of information.

The project team had been assembled in the conference room, and this time it was the archeologist's turn to address them. For three weeks Cristina Peterson had been studying the tape almost constantly, and now she was ready to give her opinion. With the exception of Jack, who had been working closely with her, they were all, even Prof. Kraft, eagerly awaiting the report. There had been a great deal of speculation about what her findings would be.

"First," she began, "before I get your hopes up, I want to say that I have not been able to get a word for word translation of the voice on the tape. The sample of speech is just too brief for that to be possible. If the scene had contained more action, I might have been more successful, but we were not that fortunate. I have, however, been able to form a hypothesis based on the spoken word as well as visual clues such as facial expression, setting, and so on."

"An important point to remember is that the aliens, despite certain differences in appearance, are not too dissimilar from ourselves. They are bipedal, intelligent, and possess opposable thumbs. They have binocular vision and a form of color perception as well. Brain size is about the same in relationship to total body size as in humans, and I would be greatly surprised if they were much larger or smaller than ourselves. That much can be guessed on the basis of physiology from the picture and the nature of the signal. From this information, I think that we can draw the conclusion that their planet is, within limits, earthlike."

"Probably more relevant is their state of culture. They obviously have a technology and one that is recognizable in terms of our own. That we can receive their signals is proof of that. Also, they speak, they wear clothing, we can even guess at the purpose of some of the objects visible in the tape. I might add that this is more than we can do for some of the artifacts of primitive human cultures. In some ways we have more in common with the aliens than we do with the Tasadi or Bushman."

"I want you to bear in mind that these beings are not greatly different from ourselves. If we are to properly analyze the contents of the message, we must remember that they are influenced by the same drives and forces as humans." There was an uneasy shifting in their seats on the part of the team members as they took in the meaning of her statement.

"If we accept this premise, and replace the alien with a human, we can make an educated guess as to what we are seen on the tape. I'll run it again for you so that you can make the substitution." Jack tapped the switch, and for the next minute and a half they watched the now familiar scene replay itself.

"Before I give my own opinion, would anyone else like to make a guess?" Cristina asked.

Kraft looked around the room, but it appeared as though no one had the courage to be the first to put his own views forward. To break the silence he said, "It's only a guess, but to start the discussion, I'd say that the alien might be a lecturer. He's obviously standing at some sort of podium or speaker's table."

"He seems a little too impassioned for a lecturer, at least in the physical sciences," one of the grad students remarked. "I've never seen you that excited before a class." Kraft smiled at the reference to his own low keyed classroom delivery.

"Maybe it's a political science class. They get more aroused."

Bill Warden broke in, "Why a class? It looks to me more like he's a politician trying to persuade the voters. He must be up for reelection. The sign in back could be an election poster." That brought a couple of laughs and a few less than serious comments.

"We've all had a crack at it," Prof. Kraft said. "You obviously have your own interpretation, and I think that we've been kept in suspense long enough. From the look on Jack's face, it must be a good one. Let's hear it now. After all, the communication between two species is one of the most important events in human history."

She smiled at the jibe. "All your suggestions are plausible, but I've spent more time analyzing the tape than you have. I'll play it again for you and point out the features that have led me to my interpretation."

"The first thing that caught my attention was the fact that the word 'gratach' was mentioned fourteen times, an unusually high incidence in such a brief speech. Furthermore, at least four of those times the speaker pointed to the symbols on the chart behind him. I think that we can assume that 'gratach' is a name, and the symbols form the written version."

"Now here's something that I want you to see." She froze the picture on the television. "Note the artifacts on the table, a bowl filled with a substance and a box or container. There appears to be some writing on the box, but the resolution of the picture isn't good enough to allow us to make it out. However," she said as the tape began to roll again, "as the alien points to the box and says 'gratach' it is likely that the symbols again spell out the name in the chart behind the alien. Note, too, the expression on his face. Despite the lack of a nose, the face is surprisingly human, and if that expression was on a human face, it would be one of approval or pleasure."

"I think that if you put all the clues together, you can come to only one conclusion. Dr. Warden was not far off when he suggested a political campaign. The speaker is definitely trying to persuade his audience, but it is the package, not himself, that he is trying to sell."

"Oh, god," Kraft sputtered. "You can't mean it. The first communication from another planet and it's only . . ."

"Yes, I'm afraid so," Cristina said. "The first and only signal received from another world is nothing more than a breakfast food commercial."

Also From Resurrected Press
SCIENCE FICTION AUTHORS RESURRECTED

FYFE RESURRECTED - THE STORIES OF H. B. FYFE

Stories from the Golden Age of Science Fiction by the author of D-99. dealing with the interaction of humans and aliens on far off worlds in ways that were as creative as they were imaginative.

SCHMITZ RESURRECTED - SELECTED STORIES OF JAMES H. SCHMITZ

Includes "An Incident on Route 12", "Watch the Sky", "The Other Likeness", "The Star Hyacinths", "Oneness", "The Winds of Time", "Ham Sandwich" and "Gone Fishing".

SHECKLY RESURRECTED - THE EARLY STORIES OF ROBERT SHECKLEY

Resurrected Press has collected some of the best of these from the 50's including "Warrior Race", "The Leech", "Watchbird", "Warm", "Diplomatic Immunity", "The Hour of Battle", "Besides Still Waters", "Keep Your Shape", "One Man's Poison", 'Ask a Foolish Question", "Cost of Living", "Death Wish Forever".

DICK RESURRECTED - THE EARLY STORIES OF PHILIP K. DICK

Early stories from the author of the novels that inspired "Blade Runner," "Total Recall," and "A Scanner Darkly".

HAMILTON RESURRECTED - CLASSIC STORIES OF EDMOND HAMILTON

Edmond Hamilton was one of the most popular writers during the 30's and 40's, the period that saw the first flowering of modern science fiction.

SMITH RESURRECTED - SELECTED STORIES OF EVELYN E. SMITH

During an era when women rarely appeared in science fiction magazines, Evelyn E. Smith appeared regularly in the pages of Galaxy and Fantastic Universe. Resurrected Press is proud to return these stories to print.

NOURSE RESURRECTED - THE WORKS OF ALAN E. NOURSE

Alan E. Nourse was both a physician and a writer. He produced most of his work in that period known as the "Golden Age of Science Fiction. Best known for his novel Star Surgeon, he was also a prolific author of short stories during the 50's. This collection includes some of his best from that era including "Derelict," "The Coffin Cure," "Bear Trap," "Contamination Crew" and more.

LEINSTER RESURRECTED - SCIENCE FICTION STORIES FROM THE 1950's

For over five decades, Murray Leinster was one of the most respected names in science fiction. Though he began writing at the dawn of the pulp era his work evolved with the times. The ten stories collected here appeared during the 50's, that "Golden Age" of the genre. Spanning the gamut from alien invasions to alternate realities, they form a fitting display of his talents in what was his fourth decade as a writer.

OTHER CLASSIC SCIENCE FICTION NOVELS FROM RESURRECTED PRESS

TALENTS, INCORPORATED - BY MURRAY LEINSTER
When a Mekinese fleet conquers his home planet, Captain Bors turns to Talents, Incorporated for help using their collection of individuals with unusual abilities to defeat the enemy and save the galaxy.

THE PIRATES OF ERSATZ - BY MURRAY LEINSTER
Bran Hodden just wanted to be an electronic engineer and marry a delightful girl. But when he's framed by the powers on Walden he's forced to turn back to his family's trade, piracy. Also published as The Pirates of Zan.

EMPIRE - BY CLIFFORD SIMAK
Spencer Chambers and Interplanetary Power owned the Solar System because they controlled the source of power. It fell to Russell Page and Harry Wilson to challenge that control if they had to cross the universe to do it.

NIGHT OF THE LONG KNIVES - THE CREATURE FROM THE CLEVELAND DEPTHS - BY FRITZ LEIBER
Two classic novellas set in the not too distant future from a classic master of science fiction.

POLICE YOUR PLANET - BY LESTER DEL RAY
Of all the cities on all the planets of the Solar System, Marsport was the most corrupt. So when one-time prize-fighter, cop, and reporter, Bruce Gordon ends up with a one way ticket to Mars, it was only natural that he would find himself walking a beat collecting graft like the rest of the force. Just trying to survive, he finds himself caught in the middle between two rival gangs as they battle for control of the planet.

The Fictional Detective
by Greg Fowlkes

Who killed Ezekial O. Handler?

A beautiful dame, a hard-boiled private eye — and a dead body.

It started like any other case. When a famous writer dies in a mysterious car crash, private detective Frank Slade is called in to find answers, but all he finds is more questions.   Who killed Ezekial Handler? Who is Janet Nielsen and why is she so interested in finding out? Who is leaving the neatly typed clues? And as Slade tries to find answers to these questions he starts to wonder if the ultimate answer will threaten his very existence.

Read about it in
The Fictional Detective

Visit www.thefictionaldetective.com

About Resurrected Press

A division of Intrepid Ink, LLC, Resurrected Press is dedicated to bringing high quality, vintage books back into publication. See our entire catalogue and find out more at www.ResurrectedPress.com.

About Intrepid Ink, LLC

Intrepid Ink, LLC provides full publishing services to authors of fiction and non-fiction books, eBooks and websites. From editing to formatting, from publishing to marketing, Intrepid Ink gets your creative works into the hands of the people who want to read them. Find out more at www.IntrepidInk.com.